MARVEL

# MILES MORALES
## SPIDER-MAN

**MARVEL**

# MILES MORALES
# SPIDER-MAN

*by Jason Reynolds*

**MARVEL**

LOS ANGELES • NEW YORK

First Edition, August 2017

3 5 7 9 10 8 6 4

FAC-020093-17228

Printed in the United States of America

This book is set in 11.5-pt Sabon LT Std, Minion Pro, Helvetica Neue LT Pro/ Monotype; Barkpipe/Fontspring.
Designed by Maria Elias

Library of Congress Control Number: 2016915216
ISBN 978-1-4847-8748-9

Reinforced binding

Visit www.hyperionteens.com
www.marvel.com

SUSTAINABLE FORESTRY INITIATIVE  Certified Sourcing  www.sfiprogram.org  SFI-00993

THIS LABEL APPLIES TO TEXT STOCK

FOR ALLEN

*We wear the mask that grins and lies,*
*It hides our cheeks and shades our eyes,—*
*This debt we pay to human guile;*
*With torn and bleeding hearts we smile,*
*And mouth with myriad subtleties.*

—Paul Laurence Dunbar, from
"We Wear the Mask"

## CHAPTER ONE

**M**iles set the good dishes on the table. The white porcelain with the blue detailing glazed over the top—ornate flowers and intricate images of old Chinese villages that nobody in his family had ever been to. *Good china*, his father called it, passed down from his grandmother only to be used on Sundays and special occasions. And though it was Sunday, today was also a special occasion for Miles, because it was the last day of his punishment.

"My suggestion to you, mijo, is that you make sure you get it all out before his class," Miles's mother said, lifting a window and fanning the smoke from the stove out with a hand towel. "Because I swear, if you get suspended again for something like this, it's gonna be you I'm fanning out the window."

Miles was suspended for having to pee. Well, for *saying* he had to pee. After his history teacher, Mr. Chamberlain, said no, Miles begged. And once Mr. Chamberlain said no again, Miles left. So he was actually suspended for leaving class. But here's the thing—Miles didn't really have to pee. And no, he didn't have to do *that* either. Miles had to rescue someone.

At least he thought he did. Truth was, his spider-sense had been on the fritz lately. But Miles couldn't risk it—couldn't ignore what he considered his responsibility.

"I don't always have time to pee before class, Ma," Miles replied. He rinsed forks and knives in the sink, while his mother hung the towel on the oven handle. She grabbed a pair of tongs and lifted chunks of chicken breast from the sizzling grease.

"Yeah, you used to say that every night, and guess what? You wet the bed more than any boy I've ever seen."

"The boy could've set a record," Miles's father chimed in from the couch. He was flipping through Friday's *Daily Bugle*. He only got the Friday edition; his theory was that if he were to actually read it each day, he'd never leave the house. Creatures everywhere were threatening civilization—and those were just the articles about reality TV. "Miles, I swear you were the most bed-wettingest kid in Brooklyn. Matter fact, back then I used to get this trash paper every morning, just so we could line the top of your mattress with it in the evening." Mr. Davis closed the paper, folded it in half. He shook his head. "And *then* your pissy butt would come waddling into our bedroom in the middle of the night smelling like two-hundred-year-old lemonade, talkin' 'bout, *I had an accident.* An *accident?* I'ma tell you right now, son, be thankful for your mother, because if it were up to me, you would've been lying in the wet spot until it was a dry spot."

"Be quiet, Jeff," Miles's mother said, positioning the chicken on a serving plate.

"Am I lying, Rio? You were always savin' him."

"Because he's my baby," she said, laying a paper towel on the first layer of meat to sop the grease from the glistening skin. "But you not *a* baby no more. So figure out what you need to do to keep your butt in that seat."

Miles had already made up his mind that that wouldn't be a problem. He was going to stay in his seat in Mr. Chamberlain's class and ignore his beehive brain whenever the bees up there got to buzzing. His spidey-sense had always been his alarm, the thing that let him know when there was danger close, or when someone needed help. But since the beginning of this school year, his junior year at Brooklyn Visions Academy, his spidey-sense seemed to be . . . broken. Almost like his powers were wearing off. He'd been dashing out of Chamberlain's class over and over again for fake bathroom breaks, bolting down the hallway and out the door, a gust of wind, only to find . . . nothing. No monster. No mutant. No madman. Just Brooklyn being Brooklyn, left with a new awkward excuse about what took him so long in the bathroom.

Perhaps, for a kid like him, being a Super Hero had an expiration date. And it wasn't worth being punished by his folks—it wasn't worth failing a class, or being expelled—if he couldn't even guarantee he'd still be able to be Spider-Man by graduation.

The buzzer buzzed just as Miles finished setting the table for four. He scooted past his mother, who was scooping yellow rice from a pot into a bowl, and stuck his head out the open window.

"I don't know why you look to see who it is like you don't already know," Miles's father said, washing his hands in the sink. He kissed Miles's mother loudly on the cheek. "Smells good, baby. Matter fact, it smells so good that our son's knucklehead friend could smell it on the other side of Brooklyn."

"Be nice. You know he's going through some changes," Miles's mother said.

"We going through some changes, too—nickels, dimes, and quarters." Miles's father rubbed his thumb and index fingers together. "I'm just sayin', I love the kid, but we can't really afford another mouth at this table."

Miles's mother faced his father, placed her hands on his chest, and sighed. "Love is deed, papi. Not just fine phrases." She planted a peck on his lips.

"Yo!" Miles, grossed out by his parents, yelled down to the stoop. "Hold on." On the other side of the room, Miles hit the button that automatically unlocked the front door. Then cracked the one leading into the building, the sound of heavy footfalls climbing the steps.

"Yo," Ganke said, almost falling into the apartment. Ganke, a burly Korean kid, was Miles's best friend, confidant, and roommate at Brooklyn Visions Academy. He immediately inspected Miles's face, right cheek, left cheek, then whispered, "You okay? I'm surprised your folks didn't kill you," before moving past Miles to greet his parents. "Hey, Mrs. M., Mr. Jeff. What's for din-din?"

"I'm not sure, Ganke, but guess who would know? *Your* parents," Miles's father said. Mrs. Morales slapped her husband on the arm.

"Oh, I know what they're having for dinner, Mr. Jeff. I already ate it," Ganke said with a shrug.

"Um, Ganke, wash your hands and sit down. You know you're always welcome here, even if it's for dinner number two. Tonight we're having chicharrón de pollo."

Ganke sent a confused look to Miles's father, who now stood behind a chair at the head of the table. "Fried chicken," he said, his face volleying back and forth between annoyed and sympathetic.

"Oh, sweet."

"Not like it would've mattered," Miles's father jabbed, sliding out his chair and taking a seat.

"Got that right, Mr. Jeff."

Miles set the chicken, the rice, and the greens on the table, then took his seat. His mother put big spoons in the rice and greens bowls, and tongs on the chicken plate. Then she sat down as well.

"Bless the food, Jeff," Mrs. Morales said. Miles, his father, and Ganke instantly snatched their eager hands back from the bowls and spread them wide to grab hold of the person sitting next to them.

"Yep, yes, of course. Bow your heads, boys," Miles's father said. "Lord, please help our son, Miles, behave himself in school. Because if he doesn't, this very well may be the last home-cooked meal he ever has. Amen."

"Amen," Miles's mother said seriously.

"Amen!" Ganke said.

Miles sucked his teeth, shot Ganke a look. Ganke leaned in for the chicken tongs.

Sunday dinner at Miles's house was a tradition. Throughout the week Miles was away, staying on campus at the Brooklyn Visions Academy, and on Saturday, well . . . even Miles's parents knew that there wasn't a sixteen-year-old in all of Brooklyn who wanted to spend Saturday evening with his folks. But Sunday was perfect for an early family meal. A lazy day for everyone. As a matter of fact, besides his mother making him get up for early morning mass, Miles typically had the rest of the day free to loaf around and watch old sci-fi movies with his dad in the afternoon and pray his mother was making his favorite for dinner—pasteles.

But this Sunday hadn't been quite as relaxed. Nor had the rest of the weekend. After being suspended Thursday afternoon, Father Jamie down at the church would've just given Miles a few Hail Marys to make penance and sent him on his way. But "Father Jeff" gave him a few Hell Nahs and sent him to his room.

It all started Friday, when Miles had been awakened at six in the morning and dragged outside on the stoop by his father.

"What are we doing out here, Dad?" Miles asked. He was wearing a wrinkled BVA T-shirt, holey sweatpants, and flip-flops. Trash cans and stuffed bags lined the block, some torn open by stray cats searching for scraps, others rummaged through by canners who sneaked around at night, looking for cans and bottles to trade in for dimes and quarters.

His father didn't answer him, at least not right away. Just sat there on the top step, holding a napkin, sipping a cup of coffee.

"So . . . about this suspension." Sip, swallow. "What exactly happened?" There was steel in his voice.

"Well, um, it was . . . my head was doing the . . . I had a . . . a feeling," Miles stammered. His dad also knew his secret and had been keeping it from his mother for a while now. But his father was still a . . . father. Not of Spider-Man, but of Miles Morales. He made that clear to Miles as often as possible.

"So this was about you saving somebody, huh? Yeah, well, let me ask you something, Super Hero. . . ." He took another sip from his mug. "Who's gonna save you?"

Miles just sat there, silent, searching for an answer that would satisfy his old man, while at the same time praying for anything to change the subject.

The sun had just started to rise, a line of gold streaking across the red brick of the brownstones, when a miracle happened in the form of rumbling trash trucks. *Saved*, Miles thought as he and his father shifted their attention, watching the garbagemen slowly move down the street—one driving, two walking alongside the truck sling-ing bags, dumping cans, and throwing them back onto the sidewalk. Plastic forks, chicken bones, toilet paper gaskets and other remnants that had slipped through holes in the bags were left strewn up and down the sidewalk. It had been ten minutes and Miles still had no idea what he and his old man were doing out there. Until the trash truck was done with their block.

"You know what, we'll talk about this more later. For now, son, why don't you tidy up."

"What you mean?"

Miles's father stood, stretched his legs, and took another sip. He pointed up and down the street. "See all these cans? Be a good *hero* and put them back where they belong. Helping your neighbors is the most heroic thing you can do, right?"

Miles sighed.

"Oh," his father continued. "And get up all this trash that our wonderful garbagemen left behind."

"With what?" Miles asked, instantly grossed out. He wished he had one of his web-shooters on so he wouldn't have had to actually touch, or even get close to, the plastic baggies of dog poop and fish guts. Not that he could sling web in his pajamas anyway.

"Figure it out, son."

And that was just the beginning of his punishment. After that, Miles had to clean the apartment, schlep loads of clothes to and from the Laundromat, and make dinner for himself, which ended up being Top Ramen with hot sauce and toast. Saturday, his father walked him up and down the block, knocking on doors asking neighbors if there was anything they needed done. He got stuck dragging an old mattress out of Ms. Shine's basement—where her junkie son, Cyrus, used to live—hanging pictures in Mr. Frankie's house, and walking all the neighborhood dogs that needed walking. Which meant there was poop that needed bagging. Lots of it.

And on and on with the neighborhood "heroics." Chore after chore. Job after job. Ramen pack after ramen pack.

Now, over Sunday dinner, Miles shuddered at the memory and reached for a second helping of rice and another piece of chicken. For the first Sunday in a long time he was out-eating Ganke and his father. And that wasn't just because of the delicious flavor of his mother's cooking. But also because of the sweet taste of his punishment—his torture—finally being over.

Until Miles's father chose to douse the dinner with current affairs.

"Read in the paper earlier that kids are getting beaten up and robbed for their sneakers," his father said, randomly. He pushed greens into his mouth, chewed, swallowed. "I'm talking to you, Ganke."

"Me?"

"Yeah."

"Well, I haven't had no problems. Just walked here from the train like I always do, and nobody seemed to care," Ganke said.

Miles's father leaned to the side to check out Ganke's

sneakers. "No, I'm thinking maybe you're the one stealing shoes."

"Ha!" Miles's mother yipped, pushing herself out from the table. She put her plate in the sink and threw over her shoulder, "You know Ganke couldn't hurt a fly. Miles couldn't either." Ganke and Miles's father both flashed a quick glance at Miles. His dad made a funny face at him at the same time his mom turned around. "Jeff," she huffed, catching him in the act. "It's like I'm raising *two* boys. Matter fact, just for that, *you* washing dishes."

"No I'm not," Miles's father said like a disobedient child. He chuckled, and set his fork down on the plate. "Your baby, Miles, is gonna do that. Call it punishment dessert. A cherry on top." Ganke blew a raspberry. Miles gave him a stone face. "Or, son, we can trade if you like. I'll do the dishes, and you pay all those bills over there," he added, pointing to the stack of envelopes rubber-banded on the coffee table.

"I know," Miles groaned. He knew what was coming next.

"And like I always say, *it takes wages, not wishes, to stop washing dishes.*" Miles's father added, "*And* you gon' take out the trash."

After dinner, Miles grabbed the trash bag, ran down the stoop, and tossed it into the can. When he turned around his dad was sitting on the top step, the same step where he'd sat on Friday. It was like a game of Simon Says, except with Jeff. *Jeff says sit down, Miles. Jeff says don't talk until I ask you a question, Miles.*

Neither of them said a word for a minute, the silence sizzling in Miles's stomach, as if the chicken he had just eaten were refrying itself.

"You know me and your mother love you," his father said, finally.

"Yeah." Miles could feel the setup coming.

"And you gettin' ready to go back to school, so listen, I need you to understand. . . . I just need you to, like . . ." Miles's father was the one doing the stammering now, searching for the right words. Finally, he just shot it straight. "You know your uncle was suspended. A lot." Miles's father pressed his hands together. "He didn't think he ever had to follow rules. And it got him killed. And the last thing your mother and I want is for you to be . . . like him."

*You're just like me.*

The words pierced Miles, lodged in his neck. *Suspended. Rules. Killed.* Miles swallowed hard, washed his guilt down with confusion. He was used to his uncle being brought up in times like these, but it stung every time. In fact, the *only* time Uncle Aaron was brought up was when his father was trying to explain to him all the ways *not* to be. His father and uncle were street kids—Brooklyn jack-boys—who were always robbing and hustling, going in and out of court and juvie until they were old enough to go in and out of jail. Miles's father met his mother and ended up choosing a different path, but his uncle Aaron kept chasing fast money in dark alleys. Now Uncle Aaron was the standard for stupid, the example for all things wrong in their family, as far as Miles's dad was concerned.

"You understand?" Miles's father asked.

Miles sat there gnawing on the inside of his cheek, thinking about Uncle Aaron. What he knew about him. Not just what he had been told by his father over and over and over again. But what he knew firsthand—that he was there when his uncle was killed. That three years ago, Uncle Aaron had accidentally killed himself while trying to kill Miles.

"I understand."

## CHAPTER TWO

**M**iles rolled the mask down over his forehead, over his eyes. For a split second, darkness. Then he lined up the holes so his vision cleared and continued stretching it over his nose, mouth, and chin. He looked at himself in the mirror. Spider-Man. Then he rolled the mask back up, again, that quick moment of darkness. He'd been doing this—the back-and-forth with it—for a few minutes. Miles's father had told him time and time again that when he and Uncle Aaron were young, they used to take their mother's dark stockings and pull them over their heads, cut the rest of the leg part off and tie it in a knot before pulling robberies. He said it was uncomfortable, and took a second to get used to, like being trapped in some kind of cocoon. "Aaron didn't become no butterfly, though," he would say. "He became something else."

*You're just like me.*

Uncle Aaron lived in the Baruch Houses, a few blocks from a Ray's Pizza. Baruch was a huge housing development running along Franklin D. Roosevelt Drive. Right on the East River. If it weren't for the fact that there were over five thousand people living in fifteen blocks of brick high-rises, it might've been considered prime real estate. Waterfront property. Miles would always meet Uncle Aaron on the corner of East Houston and Baruch Place at a bodega, where Aaron would buy grape soda. Then they'd go and get a whole pizza, before walking through the forest of skyscrapers to get back to Uncle Aaron's apartment. Because you never walk through projects by yourself unless you live there.

If Miles's parents had known that he used to spend time with Uncle Aaron, he'd be on punishment for the rest of his life. As in, forty years old with kids of his own, still not allowed to go outside. So Miles would tell them he was going to hang out with some friends at Ray's Pizza. Which was technically true . . . even though there were like a hundred Ray's Pizzas in New York. And this "friend" was, in fact, his uncle. And Miles always made sure he wasn't in Aaron's apartment when he had to call his parents to check in, that way he wouldn't have to lie. He couldn't. It just wasn't his thing.

Uncle Aaron's apartment—4D—had nothing in it but a mattress, a few fold-up chairs, a rickety TV stand with a TV on top, and a small coffee table with a few packs of panty hose on it. There was also always random shoe boxes, size nine, which Miles knew was too small for his uncle, and he hated the fact that they were also too small for him. Probably just merch to be boosted on the block. *Fell off the trucks.*

Everything else, like all of Aaron's clothes and things, were in trash bags lined up along the wall. He was all the way moved in—as a matter of fact, this was the only place Miles had ever known Aaron to live—but always seemed like he was ready to move out.

While Miles and Uncle Aaron ate, sitting on the fold-out chairs with the pizza box on the empty corner of the coffee table, they talked about family, school, and girls. Well, really Uncle Aaron would talk about girls, but he'd do it in a way that made Miles feel like *they* were talking about girls, even though Miles really didn't have nothing to say about them besides *I don't really have nothin' to say about them.* The one thing Uncle Aaron never—NEVER—talked to Miles about was "business." He never told him about the banks, or the stores he had hit. He never talked about how he'd stalk around Wall Street, the only late-night ghost town in New York, waiting to catch unassuming, stiff-suited stockbrokers working over-time. And he definitely didn't tell Miles about the biggest hit of all, the one he made just before Miles came for a visit one afternoon. The one that would change Miles's life, and ruin their relationship. OSBORN Industries. The home of the most cutting-edge innovation when it came to defense, biomedical, and chemical technologies. And spiders. Genetically mutated, chemically enhanced spiders.

It was forty-five minutes before Miles would have to leave to make the phone call home. TV playing midday talk shows. *Are you ready to see her new makeover?! Gina, come on out!* A duffel bag on the floor next to Miles's chair, full of money and pieces of technology Aaron thought he could sell on the black market. And from the bag emerged a spider, one that crawled up the leg of the chair and bit Miles right on the top of his hand, sending a sizzle down to his fingertips.

"Ouch!" Miles hissed, flicking the spider onto the floor. Uncle Aaron jumped up and stomped it dead.

"Sorry, kid," he said, with absolutely no embarrassment in his voice. He smeared the spider on the wood floor like chewing gum on the sidewalk. Miles saw him square himself to get a look at the guts. The goo that was aglow. "But you know how it is. Baruch ain't no brownstone."

There was a bang on the bathroom door.

Miles instantly camouflaged, blending in with the Pepto-pink tile of the wall.

"Miles? You fall in, son?" his mother shouted. After he'd come back in from taking out the trash and getting the *You know your uncle was this and that* talk, he'd left his parents and Ganke in the living room. His father, opening mail—mainly bills—from the day before. His mother, flipping through TV channels looking for Lifetime. And Ganke, a belly full of chicken and rice, sitting on the couch, waiting for Miles so they could get going back to Brooklyn

Visions Academy. Miles shook his head and came out of camo mode—he was way too on edge.

"Um, no!" Miles yelled. "I'll be out in a second. Just, um . . . brushing my hair." He knew she wouldn't believe that. It was the one time he took comfort in knowing she probably assumed he was having some . . . alone time. Miles pulled off the mask and used his hand to try to smooth his hair down.

"Rio!" his father called. "Come see this!"

"Hurry up, Miles. I don't want y'all leaving too late. You heard what your father said about those punks robbing kids." His mother walked away from the door, zipping a "What is it?" to his father.

Miles listened for his mother's retreat before dashing across the hall to his bedroom. He stuffed the mask into his backpack and grabbed his brush off the table so he could keep up with the whole *hair-brushing* story.

"Aight, I'm ready," Miles said, entering the living room acting like he hadn't been in the bathroom forever. *Brush, brush, brush.* The top goes forward, down on the left, down on the right, down in the back. In that order. His mother was standing beside the couch reading a piece of mail that she pressed to her chest once Miles walked in the room. Miles figured it was another bill—there was always another bill. If he asked about it, he would just trigger another lecture about how important it was that he do well in school. And after the last three days he'd had, he couldn't take another one of those.

"All that brushing ain't gon' get it, son," his father said, tapping Miles's mother on the leg to snap her out of her trance. "Rio."

Startled, she folded the letter, stuffed it back in the envelope, and handed it back to Miles's father.

"Um . . . sorry," she said, approaching Miles. She ran her palm along his head. "You need a haircut, papi."

"This weekend when you come home, we're going to the barbershop. Can't have you out here woofin'," his father teased.

Miles kept brushing his hair and brushed his parents off. "You ready?" he asked Ganke, who had gotten up from the couch and flung his backpack over his shoulder, a goofy grin spread across his face. Ganke always loved these moments with Miles and his family. More ammo for jokes.

"Yep. Take care, Mrs. M." Ganke came in for a hug.

"Bye, Ganke. Keep him in line, please."

"I always try, but the boy's crazy."

"Whatever, man," Miles said, hugging his mother and kissing her on the cheek.

"Mr. Jeff." Ganke reached out his hand. Miles's father took it, squeezed it tight. Ganke's face wrinkled with pain.

"Next Sunday we're having an all-veggie dinner. You in?"

"You know it!" Ganke chimed.

Miles's father looked at his mother, shook his head. "I tried, honey. But it didn't work." He laughed.

"Okay, okay, you boys be safe, please. Ganke, tell your mother I said hello. Miles, call us when you get there."

"Of course." He slipped his brush in his bag.

"Don't forget, mijo."

"I won't."


Once outside, Miles was about to ask Ganke how his weekend had gone, especially since he knew time at home had been weird for Ganke since his parents had split up. But Ganke had a way of sensing those kinds of awkward questions, so before Miles could get it out, Ganke countered with a doozy of his own.

"So there's something I've been meaning to ask you for, like, ever." Ganke had just finished tying his shoes at the bottom of Miles's stoop. Miles took the concern on the tip of his tongue and slipped it underneath it, like gum—to be saved for later. Miles knew Ganke was probably setting him up for some joke he'd been thinking about for the last thirty minutes. He was one of those friends you couldn't leave alone with your parents because he would ask all kinds of ridiculous questions, digging for secret embarrassing things that your mother and father would see as cute. Stuff like *Miles used to cry every Martin Luther King Jr. Day. Not because of what happened to Dr. King, but because the television and radio would play clips of his speeches and Miles always thought he sounded like a ghost. Or Miles had irritable bowel syndrome and crapped his pants until he was ten.*

"What?" Miles groaned as they passed Ms. Shine's house. He remembered the way that mattress smelled when he'd moved it out for her, the way it felt to have those mystery stains and globs of matted white cat hair brush against his cheek. *Ugh.*

"Aight, don't get mad," Ganke prepped Miles, "but . . ."

"Just say it."

"Okay, so . . . your last name. It don't really make sense to me."

"What? Morales?"

"Yeah."

"I'm half–Puerto Rican."

Ganke stopped walking and twisted his face up at Miles, like *Duh.*

"So . . ."

"So, your *mother's* name is Rio Morales, right?"

"Correct."

"And your father's name is Jefferson Davis."

"Two for two."

"So then why isn't your name Miles Dav—" Ganke's eyes widened. "Oh . . . snap. *Miles Davis!*" He stopped walking again, this time in front of Mr. Frankie's house. Ganke folded himself in half, exploding into laughter. "Wait . . . wait!" He tried to catch his breath while Miles laser-stared him down. "Miles. I'm sorry. Wait . . . Miles Davis? I just . . . I never thought of that until just now. . . . Oh . . . man . . . hold on. . . ." The laughter tapered off. "Okay . . . *woo.* Okay . . ."

"You done?"

"I'm done. I'm so done. Sorry, man, it just caught me off guard." They continued down the block.

"Anyway, that's not even the reason," Miles said. "But I'm glad you think that's so funny."

"So then, why?"

"Ganke, why you actin' like you don't know my mother? Better yet, why you actin' like you don't know my abuela?" Now Miles laughed. "Nah, seriously, I don't know. I kind of think it's something else."

"Like what?"

Miles shrugged. "Back in the day, my pops and my uncle did enough dirt in their lives to make Davis a bad word in some circles. I look just like them both and live in the same neighborhood, so, I don't know, I wonder. . . ."

"Gotcha," Ganke said, the funny finally all faded.

There was an empty quarter-water jug on the sidewalk. They were shaped like small plastic barrels, but Miles always pretended they were grenades when he was younger. He kicked it, and it rolled ahead in front of him. He cleared his throat. "That's also why I think my superpowers are messin' up."

"Uh . . . you think they're messing up because of your last name?" Ganke asked.

"No. But because of what my last name *means*. I mean, what that part of me is. Like, what if I'm not cut out to be . . . I don't know . . . good?"

It all just made so much sense to him. Like how really tall people usually have really tall parents. Or how you can be predisposed to be an alcoholic if one of your parents is. Miles had what he always considered complicated genetics: *bad* blood. And, to make it worse, his father and uncle were sixteen when they got started in crime, which was Miles's age now. So maybe that part of his bloodline was fighting whatever changes to it the spider bite had caused, like some kind of grimy blood cell fighting off anything awesome inside him.

"Dude, shut up."

"I'm serious, man."

"You're also stupid. Like, that's just silly. That's like saying if you play basketball, your kids are gonna play."

"Good chance," Miles said. He used his thumb and index finger as a pincer claw to pick up the empty jug he'd kicked, residual responsibility from Friday's trash cleanup.

"When's the last time you've seen Michael Jordan Jr.?"

"I'm not sure if Michael Jordan has a junior, Ganke." Miles tossed the grenade in a neighbor's open garbage bin.

"Exactly. And do you know *why* you don't know if Jordan has a little Jordan?" Ganke asked. "Because Little Jordan didn't grow up to be . . . Little Jordan." Miles didn't reply. "I mean, you don't even know why your buzzy head-alarm thingy is all outta whack. Might be because . . . it's just wearing off. Like maybe the super stuff from the spider venom, or whatever, was like a virus that took a few years to finally pass through your system. Or maybe it's just hiccuping because you're growing. Shoot, for all we know, you could mess around and lose *all* your superpowers when you finally get a girlfriend!" Ganke's jaw dropped.

"Sounds like something my uncle would've said." Miles stepped over a pile of dog crap.

"Lucky for you, the girlfriend thing ain't happening no time soon," Ganke fired off, tapping Miles on the arm.

"Yeah, for you either!" Miles shot back.

"Look, the point I'm making is, true, you don't know what's causing it, but worrying about it probably isn't helping. You gotta de-stress. Relax a little bit. Have some fun with it." Ganke sent a wave through his arm as if he were breakdancing. "Shoot, if I had what you have . . ."

"Man, what? What would you do?" Miles asked, his tone short and sharp.

Ganke stopped walking for the third time. The train station was to the right. Ganke peered down the street, then looked left to make sure no cars were coming. "Let's go straight, and I'll show you."

Two blocks to the basketball court. When they got there, a two-on-two was in play.

"What we doing here?" Miles asked as he and Ganke strolled up to the gate.

"Just a little pit stop. You asked me what I would do."

"Ah. Maybe next time, man," Miles said, peering through the gate. "They're already runnin' a game." But Ganke wasn't having it.

"Let's go." Ganke headed in.

"Nah, man." Miles grabbed his arm.

"Come on. It'll be fun."

"Ganke, I—"

"Hey, guys! Guys!" He walked onto the court, strutted right into the middle of the game. Miles followed behind him but stopped at the sideline.

"Time-out, time-out!" Ganke called, jamming the fingers of one hand into the palm of the other, making a *T*.

"Yo, what you doin'?" a short guy with a puffed-up chest asked, picking up his dribble. "You not playin', so you can't call time-out. Matter fact, you can't call nothin'." He flared his nostrils. Miles shook his head. He wasn't in the mood for a fight and couldn't risk having his eye blacked or anything like that.

"Get off the court, Bruce Bruce Lee," the short guy said.

"Who is Bruce Bruce Lee? You mean, *Bruce* Lee?" Ganke said.

The guys all looked around at each other, bewildered. "You don't know who Bruce Bruce is? The comedian?" Shorty Puff-Chest put his arms out and blew out his cheeks to do his best and worst imitation of a fat person. "Fat funnyman. And Lee, because—"

"Because that's my last name," Ganke deadpanned. Miles stifled a laugh.

"Wait . . . your last name Lee, forreal?" Shorty Puff-Chest asked.

"Yep. And *his* name"—Ganke pointed back at Miles— "is Miles Davis." Miles sighed, rolling his eyes.

"Like the jazz dude?"

"Nah, like the dude who's about to take your money," Ganke cracked.

"Oh, word?" Another one of the guys spoke up. He was light-skinned, the color of flu mucus. And slimy, too, from sweat. "And how he gon' do that?"

"Dunk contest."

"Wait . . . *what*?" Miles squawked, now stepping timidly onto the court.

Mucus Man smiled and tapped the dude standing next to him. A man built like . . . well . . . like a Super Hero spoke up.

"Now you talkin' my language. I don't know if you know who I am, but ain't too many cats around here can out-jump me," he bragged.

"Yeah, Benji got bunnies. Jump out the gym." Mucus Man played hype-man.

"No doubt. And little jazzman over there look like he ain't even got nut-fuzz yet. He also look like he ain't got no money." The last guy on the court finally chimed in. He'd been standing off to the side drinking water. He was . . . a bear. Not an actual bear, but not far from one either.

"He don't." And as soon as Ganke said it, the guys laughed and shooed him and Miles away like pesky flies. "But," Ganke added, "I'll bet these." Ganke slipped out of his sneakers. "Air Max 90s. Infrareds. OGs. Apparently everybody wants them, and this is my first time wearing them. They probably worth, like, three hundred." Ganke wasn't a sneakerhead, but his father was. Yeah, his dad. His two favorite hobbies were hounding Ganke about school (he and Miles's parents had that in common) and collecting rare sneakers, the bulk of which he gave to his son when he moved out, under the condition that Ganke took care of them. Of course, Ganke never had to. Because Miles took care of them for him.

"*What?*" Again, from Miles.

"What size?" the man called Benji—the one built like a Super Hero—asked.

"Size ten." Ganke, ignoring Miles, eyeballed Benji's feet. "Your size."

Benji smiled, revealing a space between each jagged tooth. He dug into his sock and pulled out a wad. His buddies reached into their own pockets, socks, bags, and put up their own cash, too. After counting out the three hundred bucks, they laid it all out on the court, placing one of the sneakers on top to keep the evening breeze from turning dollars into feathers.

Then everyone cleared out in front of the hoop to give Benji and Miles space. Benji dribbled the ball intensely, as if he were pounding a head against the pavement. Miles got the drift. He shot a glance at Ganke, who was now wearing Miles's backpack on his front. Ganke smiled, followed by his usual shrug.

"Little man probably can't even grab the net," Benji said. He held the ball in both hands, took two steps and effortlessly jammed it through the rim. No warning. No warm-up. "Should be a piece of cake."

"Or a piece of steak," Ganke said from the sidelines. Miles swung around, ice-grilled him. Ganke mouthed, *Sorry, sorry,* as Miles called for the ball. But as soon as

Benji threw it to him—zipping it as if he were shooting a fireball from his hands—Miles realized he knew very little about basketball.

He bounced the ball fumblingly, slapping at it with a stiff hand. Okay, no more dribbling. Dribbling wasn't his thing. He gripped the ball, the tips of his fingers instantly becoming sticky. It felt like there were tiny cannons firing off inside him. A tingle in his elbows and fingertips. A surge of electricity shooting down the back of his legs, throbbing in the soft spot behind his knees. And then, as if it were nothing, he took two steps, jumped eye level with the orange ring, and easily dropped the ball in.

"Yo . . ." Mucus Man said, shaking his head. That's all he said. No follow-up. The others didn't say anything, but all their faces were saying the same thing: *Yo . . .*

"Aight, little man. I see you," Benji said, taking the ball. "So let's just get this over with, forreal this time." He started from the three-point line, took off running, jumped, and turned his back toward the rim midair. Holding the ball with both hands, he brought it down between his legs, then flung it up over his head and behind him, hammering it into the net with a grunt.

"*Ungh!*" Shorty Puff-Chest repeated the grunt, again, like a good hype-man. He grabbed his chest and howled dramatically. "That was so hard you almost took *me* out!"

"*Woo!*" Mucus hooted.

"Don't get no better than that, lil' man," Benji boasted, kicking the ball over to Miles.

"Oh, it does," from Ganke.

"Yeah, whatever, Bruce Bruce. We'll see."

Miles went back to the three-point line. Again, no dribbling. He eyed the rim. But right before he was about to take a running start, Ganke, of course, waved him off.

"Hold on, hold on, hold on." He skittered to the foul line, shoeless and double-backpacked. "Listen, fellas. This is fun and all, but the truth is, we don't have all night. So, how about we just get it over with?"

"We will as soon as your man makes a fool of himself by trying to do what I just did."

"Yeah . . ." Ganke held one finger up, then pointed it at Benji. "No. How about this: if he can do the dunk you did, without all that running, we win."

"Wait," Shorty Puff-Chest spoke up. "So you saying if he can do the back dunk that Benji did, on a vertical jump, y'all win."

"Exactly. And if he can't—"

"We win, and y'all get your corny asses outta here?"

"Yep," Miles said. The whole thing had been a bad idea, but this was the only part of the bad idea that sounded like a good idea. They still had to get back to school. Miles still had to make a phone call to his parents. And even though he could say the train was messed up—because the train's *always* messed up—he didn't want to lie.

Benji looked surprised, but everyone backed off the court again as Miles stepped up to the rim. He looked up at it: the familiar webbing of the net, the rusty orange circle, the dirty glass backboard. He glanced at Ganke, then at the court goons—Shorty Puff-Chest, Mucus Man, Benji, and the Bear.

In all the movies Miles had watched, there was always some kind of pep talk or intense battle drum rhythm playing in the hero's mind in these kinds of situations, but in Miles's head, he heard silly music. Like, whistling, and the theme song to *Super Mario Bros*. Whatever. All the staring up at the rim "concentration" was just for show, anyway. After the tension in his body had built enough, Miles sprang up. He twisted in midair before spreading his legs into a full split, dropping the ball down, then drawing it up over his head and into the net with such force that veins of cracked glass traveled through the backboard.

No big deal. To Miles. Or Ganke.

But from the looks on the faces of the court goons, they might as well have just witnessed the second coming of Jordan. Or maybe the second coming of Earl "The Goat" Manigault—everyone in New York had heard the legend about how, at only 6'1", Earl had snatched a dollar bill off the top of a backboard and left change. Benji and his boys were completely stunned.

Until Ganke reached for his shoes. And the money. Then the howls turned to barks. And the astonishment turned to anger.

"What you think you doin'?" Benji pressed up on Ganke as he slipped his feet back in the sneakers and picked up the cash.

"Y'all lost. I mean . . . nobody's beating that," Ganke bragged.

"Maybe I can't beat that, but I can beat *you*. So I suggest you leave the cash."

"Y'all hustled us," Mucus Man cried. Streetballers always cry about being hustled, even though they hustle people nonstop. Nobody likes to lose.

"Oh, so it was okay for y'all to take advantage of kids, though?" Miles said. "You just couldn't resist what you thought was an easy come-up on a fresh pair of sneakers. I mean, we got *backpacks*, man." He didn't necessarily care about the money—this was all just Ganke's attempt to get him to take his mind off being Spider-Man and all the Super Hero mumbo-jumbo. But now it was about principle. About these clowns keeping their word.

"Don't matter. Leave the money, and leave with your lives."

Ganke looked at Miles, nodded. Miles shook his head. Ganke nodded again. And again, Miles shook his head.

"No."

"*What?*" Ganke now was somewhere between a nod and shake.

"Yeah, *what*?" Benji repeated. The rest of the lumpheads gathered around.

"I said no," Miles confirmed.

It's amazing how quiet the basketball court gets when things are about to go south. There's a stillness. A dead air. The streetlights had flickered on by now, and what was left of the sun was just about gone—only the faintest recognition of blue in a black sky.

"Guys, you don't have to—"

"Shut up," Benji shot back at Ganke, pointing at him. "Hold him!" Shorty Puff-Chest and Mucus Man instantly flanked Ganke, grabbing him by the arms.

"Miles!" Ganke called. But before Benji could even sucker-punch Miles's best friend, or reach for the shoes, or do whatever he was going to do, Miles had already stepped in front of him. There was a tingling just behind his kneecap. In his ears. His palms and fingertips, too.

Benji flashed that raggedy, reptilian smile—Miles could hear his mouth curve, hear the thick saliva on the back of Benji's tongue—and pushed against Miles's shoulder to move him out of the way. But as soon as his hand touched Miles, Miles grabbed it and flung Benji around, away from Ganke. Benji shook his head clear and charged, but Miles leaped over him, a clean jump clearing Benji's head. He ran toward Ganke and speared himself into a jump-kick, spreading his legs at the last minute to miss Ganke's face, but catching Mucus and Shorty straight in the jaws. It wasn't enough to hurt them bad—Miles wasn't trying to—but it was enough to get them to let go of Ganke, who then ran back to the side of the court. Benji grabbed Miles from behind, and in a flash, Miles delivered three elbows to Benji's breadbasket. *Zoop, zoop, zoop!* Benji doubled over. Miles didn't finish him. Wanted to give him a chance to chill out—call off his dogs.

Shorty stalked over, his hands up, assuming the hood boxer pose. "I don't want no trouble," Miles said, his body still firing tiny rockets through his veins. Shorty didn't respond, just continued to set up his stance, then reset it. He finally threw a jab. Miles bobbed. He threw another. Miles leaned back, moved from side to side, his arms down, letting Shorty know he didn't want to fight.

"Hit his ass!" Benji squealed, still trying to catch his breath. Shorty threw a third jab, but this one Miles caught. He grabbed Shorty's wrist with one hand and used his other one to cup the joint of Shorty's elbow so that Shorty would have no choice but to punch himself in the face. A clean fist to the nose. His own fist. Miles heard the septum snap.

"ARGH!" Shorty yelled, slapping his other hand to his face. Blood, lots of it, started pouring from his nostrils. For a moment, Miles was stuck. The sight of blood startled him—he didn't mean for the hit to be so hard.

Mucus backed off, and instead of coming for Miles, he went for Ganke. Ganke made a bumbling dash across the court, yelling at the top of his lungs, while the Bear came toward Miles.

"You have nothing to do with this, man," Miles said, trying to talk him down.

"You hustled us," he growled. Then he rocketed toward Miles. Miles, again, jumped over him and kicked him in the back of the head, using the leverage to push off and dart over to Ganke. He grabbed him under the arm like a toddler and hopped up on the fence, dragging Ganke up the metal grate with him. But not before Mucus Man grabbed the backpack. The one Ganke was wearing on his front—Miles's backpack.

"Miles!"

"No, Ganke. Don't let it go!" Miles yelled, one hand clawing the iron gate, and the other clutching the armpit of his friend. He needed that bag. His secret was in there, red and black.

"Give it to me," Mucus Man growled. "Y'all leaving *everything* here!"

"I can't . . . I can't hold it!" Ganke yelled, as Mucus Man yanked and yanked on one of the straps, the other strap pressed into the crook of Ganke's free arm like it was going to rip straight through it.

"Ganke, do *not* let that bag go!"

Ganke looked up at Miles, his face full of worry. "Miles . . ." Mucus Man tugged again and Ganke's arm dropped, the bag dropping with it.

Now loose, Miles climbed farther up the fence, yanking Ganke up with him.

"I'm sorry," Ganke panted.

"Just hold on and stay up here," Miles ordered as Ganke gripped the gate, looking down from the top. Below, Mucus Man started unzipping the bag as the rest of the goons waited like alligators in basketball shorts. They weren't going to get out of this the easy way. Miles took a deep breath, and dove into the gator pit.

## CHAPTER THREE

**"I**'m sorry."

Silence.

"Miles, forreal. I'm sorry."

More silence.

"At least you got your bag back. And we got the money, too. Those are good things, right?" Ganke and Miles sat on the B train, finally on their way back to school. Miles turned his phone off. He knew his parents would be calling, and he knew he'd have to lie—*and I couldn't get service*—so he had to make sure the phone went straight to voice mail. "Crazy thing is, I don't even think these shoes are worth this much." Ganke flipped through the money, split it and gave Miles his share.

Miles sat next to him, his bag on his lap. His knee sore. His hands bruised. The spider-bite scar itching like it always did. He kept his focus straight ahead on the subway ad slogan: IF YOU SEE SOMETHING, SAY SOMETHING. Couldn't look at Ganke or even talk to him, he was so mad. Mad at himself, mostly.

The doors opened and four kids got on. Three were definitely in high school. One, elementary. Couldn't have been older than nine.

"Good evening, ladies and gentleman," the little one announced. "Y'all know what time it is? It's showtime!"

"SHOWTIME!" the older boys shouted. Then they began dancing—ticking, waving, popping, locking, getting light. They climbed train poles, flipping back, then forward, all while avoiding kicking any rider in the face. Miles didn't even look. Most people didn't. You can always tell a tourist because they stare in amazement at showtime boys, as if they're at the circus. But when you live here, you know their tricks, their jokes, the way the talented and adorable young one is the sweet spot to the pockets of fools. When you're late and annoyed and your knuckles are bruised, there's no time for showtime.

Ganke nudged Miles as the kids clapped and the music blared from a handheld stereo. Miles stared straight ahead. IF YOU SEE SOMETHING, SAY SOMETHING.

"Thank you, ladies and gentlemen," the young one said, running up and down the train car with a hat in his hand collecting money. When he got to the end of the car, where Ganke and Miles were sitting on a cramped two-seater, Ganke took one of the dollars he and Miles had just gotten from the basketball court and put it in the hat. Miles reached over and grabbed all the money left in Ganke's hand.

"Kid . . ." he called. Little man turned around and Miles held the fistful of cash in the air. The kid's face lit up and he beelined back over.

"What you . . . ?" Ganke started, but he couldn't get it out. "Miles . . . don't . . ." Miles put his half and the rest of Ganke's half in the hat. *"Miles!"*

Then, as if it were nothing, Miles returned to his position. Straight ahead. IF YOU SEE SOMETHING, SAY SOMETHING.

"Um . . . Hi, Mrs. M. This is Ganke. . . . Yes . . . yes, I know, but see . . . Miles is . . . he's in the bathroom. Yeah . . . he's . . . I think it was the chicken. I think it messed him up."

"The train. Tell her about the train," Miles whispered from the other side of their dorm.

"And that's why I'm calling and not Miles, to tell you that we were stuck on the train. I think somebody jumped or something . . . yeah . . . and Miles had to poop the whole time, so when we finally got off . . . I mean . . . Mrs. M., I swear I've never seen someone run so fast." Ganke covered his mouth, stifling the laughter. "But we made it safely. And yes . . . *he* made it safely. Uh-huh. Okay, I'll tell him to call you when he's out. Okay, bye." Ganke tapped the screen on his phone to end the call. "Boom. That's how you do it." He pretended to drop the cell phone as if he were dropping a microphone.

"Thanks." Miles stretched his fingers, slowly squeezing air, his knuckles cracking.

"It's the least I can do."

"It's cool, man."

"Hey, I know things got a little crazy at the court, but can you at least admit that it was fun?" Ganke stood up, pulled his shirt over his head, then pulled down the white tank top he had on underneath. Miles didn't budge. Not even a smirk. "Seriously? You mean to tell me you didn't have a good time, not even when you slammed that last dunk and shattered the glass? Miles Morales, the stress box who everybody knows at this school, but nobody *really* knows, the geek with a razor-sharp hairline and the clean kicks . . . uh, most of the time . . . You didn't enjoy being the man? *Really?*"

Miles sat on his bed scratching the back of his hand. He had kicked off his shoes and pitted his big toes against each other, one on top of the other. Ganke stared expectantly at him. Waiting for it . . . waiting . . . waiting . . . until finally a smile slipped onto Miles's face.

"I knew it!" Ganke cheered after seeing the grin.

"Relax. You make it seem like dunking a basketball was a day at an amusement park. Maybe it was for you, but I'm the one who had to do all the work. Not to mention, I almost had my bag stolen and had to fight. That ain't fun."

"Okay, so maybe not the bag almost being stolen and the fighting part. But the rest of it . . . gold."

"Ganke, it—"

"Gold."

"Dude. Seriously, it—"

"Gold!"

"Okay, fine." Miles sighed. "It was gold. It was freakin' gold."

Ganke burst into laughter. "Now that we got that settled, next order of business: I need to find out who Bruce Bruce is," he said, pulling his laptop from his bag.

"Well, mine is getting in the shower. Wash Benji and the Bear off me."

Miles sidestepped Ganke and headed for his closet where he kept his shower caddy. His and Ganke's room was small, a tiny box, only a little bigger than Miles's bedroom at his folks' house. There were two twin beds, one on either side, desks in front of the beds, a closet along the back wall (with an added hook for Miles's caddy) and a poster of Rihanna on the front wall that was tacked above a small table with a television on it. Under that table, a mess of wires and video game consoles. Old-school. Nintendo. Sega. An Atari they couldn't get to work. All controllers maxing out at four buttons. They were Miles's and Ganke's fathers', passed down to their offbeat kids who had a love for eight- and sixteen-bit games. Games that were all fun and no stress. No shooters, no monsters— nothing, for Miles, that was real.

The games needed a closet of their own.

The showers were no better than the rooms. Everyone on their floor shared a big bathroom with toilets on one side, sinks in the middle, and shower stalls on the other side. Tiny cells with slimy walls. Thankfully, the bathroom was empty when Miles got there. They'd gotten back late, so most boys—at least the ones who actually took showers—had already come and gone. Miles set his caddy on one of the sinks. Looked at himself in the mirror. No marks on his face, which was all he really cared about. He knew he had to be careful to not leave evidence of fighting. His knee was a little puffy, but it was fine.

But as he put toothpaste on his toothbrush and jammed it in his mouth, Miles couldn't stop thinking about what they said about him, why they wanted to beat him and Ganke up so bad anyway. That he had hustled them. *Brush, brush, brush.* And . . . he had. He knew that he could do things they couldn't do. That there would be no way they could win the bet. He took advantage of them. *Brush, brush, brush.* And then after he took advantage of them, he beat them up. And that also wasn't right. They had a right to be mad. Everyone gets mad at hustlers, especially if you're on the victim side of the hustle. And Miles knew hustling was in his veins. *You're just like me.*

*Ugh,* he thought, splashing water on his face. *Whatever.* He turned the shower on, his flip-flops slick on the floor from a week's worth of soap scum. Someone's hair was in the drain, gluey from mixing with a piece of soap the size of a skipping stone. *It was fun, though,* Miles thought. *Even that part. That's why . . . whatever.*

When Miles got back to the room, Ganke was sitting

at his desk, flipping through a notebook, his laptop frozen on a clip of a comedy series from the nineties. Miles put on a pair of shorts and sat back on his bed to massage his knee. "So what'd I miss?" he asked, pointing at Ganke's notebook.

"Since you been in the shower?" Ganke joked. "I did some breakdancing. *Showtime!*" He rolled the top half of his body.

"Come on, man. I can't go back to class tomorrow ice-cold."

"Aight, aight." Ganke turned his chair around. "Here's your briefing. I feel like your trusty sidekick, by the way. Or your hype-man." Ganke shook his head. "Anyway, so the two days you were gone . . ." Ganke thought for a second. "One thing is, Mr. Chamberlain is crazy."

"Uh . . . yeah." They had just started their unit on the Civil War in fifth-period history. Everyone figured this was Mr. Chamberlain's favorite subject to teach, because he had been talking about it the entire month that school had been in session.

"I mean, I know you know. But he's like . . . *nuts.* So he keeps talking about how the Civil War was like this beautiful, romantic thing. He talks about it like it's a video game he loves to play. But the weirdest part was on Friday, when he finally started talking about like, y'know, the nitty-gritty stuff—slavery, and how the Confederacy didn't want to end it, and all that—he was going on about how, depending on how you look at it, slavery was kind of good for the country."

"Wait, he said that?" Miles asked, grabbing one of his web-shooters from under his bed.

"I mean, basically. You know, Chamberlain. He does the whole *talking statue* thing, acting like it's gonna make him seem smarter or whatever, but that's what I took from it." Miles fired the shooter at the TV, a wad of web turning it on. Ganke shook his head. "So lazy."

"What? I'm exhausted from saving your ass," Miles joked, shooting a splat at Ganke as if it were Silly String. "Anyway, okay, Chamberlain's trippin' as usual. Blah-blah-blah. Anything else?"

"Well, yeah. This right here." Ganke struggled to peel the web off his arm. He eventually just quit and held up his notebook.

"And what's that?"

Ganke cleared his throat, and then *pretended* to clear it. "Ahem. Ahem," he said dramatically, before leaning over and turning the TV off.

"I am a vault, a safe locked by loyalty earned by few;
tell me your secrets, whisper them to me behind enemy
    backs;
I was born this way, a vault, and your secrets will die
    when I do."

Ganke looked at Miles, nodding his head. Miles returned the look, one eye slightly closed as if he was concentrating on what Ganke just said.

"What the hell are you talkin' about, Ganke?"

41

"Did you like that?"

"Um . . . what the hell are you talkin' about, Ganke?" Miles repeated.

"It's what we've been learning in Ms. Blaufuss's class since you've been on lockdown. You liked it, right?" Ganke nodded confidently at Miles's blank face. "It's a sijo. Some kind of Korean poetry." Ganke slapped his notebook on his lap, excited. "This is the poetry of my people! This is my birthright! That's why I'm so good at it!" Miles waited for Ganke to give in to his usual jokey grin, but he didn't. Miles shot more web at the TV to turn it back on. Ganke leaned over and turned it back off. "And I named this one 'MILES MORALES IS SPIDER-MAN.'" Then the grin came.

"Not anymore," Miles said, lying back on his bed. As soon as he said it, he immediately felt a heaviness leave his body. A weight lifted.

"What?"

"I'm done," Miles said. "I mean, the powers are acting all weird anyway, and honestly, I can't afford to be Spider-Man."

"You wanna get *paid* to be Spider-Man? I mean, you do know that we—well, you—just did."

"That's not what I mean. I'm not talking about hero-for-hire or nothing like that. Look, you know how over the last few years I've gotten better at being . . . I don't even know how to say it."

"I'll say it. You got better at not being a punk? Better at not being a sucker-ass mini Mario. Now you big Mario.

42

Mario with the mushroom and the invincibility star."

Miles sat back up. "Look, I'm not scared of nobody like I'm scared of my parents. And I don't mean that, like, I'm scared they gon' do something to me. I mean, I come . . . we come from . . ." Miles couldn't find the words to finish. "Think about my dad. He don't have a degree. He didn't even graduate from high school. My mother did, but she couldn't afford college. Think about my block. Cyrus Shine, wherever he is these days. Fat Tony, who spends most of his time waiting on a hand-to-hand, sitting on his stoop talking trash to whoever walks by. Frenchie at the end of the block who works around the corner at the dollar store. She's cool, but her son, Martell, *better* make it to the league. And then Neek, from across the street. Went to the army. Went to war. Fought for the country. Got out. And now he's just . . . there. Sometimes you see him pull the curtains back and peek out, but that's about it." Miles got up from his bed, grabbed his backpack. "You know what they call me every time I go in the barbershop? Baby Einstein. Smarty Arty. Stuff like that. And they smile and give me a hookup on cuts. They ask me about girls, of course, but they also ask me about my grades. My uncle used to do the same thing." He reached in and pulled out his suit, black and shiny with red webbing. "It might sound silly to you. I don't know."

Ganke leaned forward in his chair. "Okay, Miles, um, aren't you being just a *little* dramatic? You're doing bad in one class. *One* class."

"Let me ask you something, Ganke." Miles balled up

the uniform. "Did you get in here through a lottery?"

"I don't think so."

"Are you on scholarship?"

"No," Ganke said, leaning back, folding his arms across his chest.

"If for some reason this doesn't work out, do you have another plan? Are there other options for you?"

"Miles."

"I'm just asking." Ganke hesitated, then nodded. "Exactly. You and me, we the same in a lot of ways. But this ain't one of them." He opened the closet behind his bed, tossed the suit into the corner, before shutting it again. "To have the time to be a Super Hero, you gotta have the rest of your life laid out. You can't be out there saving the world when your neighborhood ain't even straight. I just gotta be real about it."

Miles flopped back on the bed. His mind was made up. He was done. He was going to do what he knew he needed to do, starting tomorrow. Refocus.

But for the rest of the night, he was going to watch as many episodes of *American Ninja Warrior* as possible. He shot another wad of web at the TV, cutting it on for the third time, while Ganke turned back toward his desk and started scribbling in his notebook. When he was finished, he propped it up on the desk, the words written so small on the page that a normal person wouldn't have been able to make them out from across the room. But Miles could.

MILES MORALES IS A DUMBASS
What good is it to quit doing the thing that you do
    best?
Unless quitting is freedom, but what if it's not
    freedom?
What if it's just a smiling family and a prison cell?

And though Miles could see the words clearly on the page, he also could see that Ganke couldn't understand how he felt. So Miles just shook his head and turned back to the TV, watching another man jump through an obstacle course to prove—for no reason at all—that he too was a little bit more than normal.

## CHAPTER FOUR

**M**iles had been to this place before. Knew it the way he knew his own house. But this was far from home. Pillars the size of trees in fantasy forests. White stone. Marble. Big wooden door with a brass ring in the middle. A castle entrance. Fountain in front of the steps. Off-white linen curtains at the windows, pulled back and tied off. Inside, leather couches like giant thrones, oak tables, tile floors far nicer than the crummy ones in Brooklyn bathrooms. Portraits on the wall of old white men. Dark paintings that made the whole house look sepia. A crystal chandelier. A grandfather clock. A cattle iron and a cat-o'-nine-tails as decoration. The smell, familiar. The fight, even more so.

Left, left, duck. Left hook, duck. Clean right uppercut to Miles's chin. He bit down on his tongue. Penny-flavored blood filled his mouth, and before he could recover there was a foot in his chest knocking him back, his body banging against the massive front door. Then came the rush. A flurry of fists. Miles did his best to block as many as he could before grabbing a lamp off the side table next to him—the lampshade made of red, green, and purple stained glass—and cracking it over the head of . . . *who?* It was as if the person he was fighting was blurred. As if there were some sort of invisible heavy plastic between them, distorting the figure. The glass from the lamp shattered, an explosion of shards as brightly colored as sundae sprinkles. The person Miles was fighting hit the floor and Miles shot some web to trap him there, but the blur dodged it, rolling backward up onto his feet, white silken cord flying from his wrist as well. *What? How?* Miles bobbed, then charged the—*web-slinging?*—blur, spearing him back into an old cabinet full of crystal trinkets. Blood dripped down his distorted face and onto the mosaic tile floor. Miles punched him. The blur punched back, and the two traded blows until finally Miles released more webbing, anticipating his combatant's next move. As expected, the blurred fighter dodged it, the web attaching itself to the old wooden cabinet—all part of the plan. Miles wound the web around his wrist and grabbed it, yanking the bureau down, a cacophony of clinking as the crystal trinkets tipped. The blurry battler quickly turned around to stop it from falling on him, and that's when Miles used the shooter on his other hand to web up the fighter's beclouded legs. *Distract and defeat.*

"It's over," Miles said, watching the man struggle to get free. Miles unloaded what seemed like a never-ending stream of webbing until his adversary was trapped in what looked like a white sleeping bag. The blur didn't respond, just rolled his head around as Miles bent over him, pushing his hands into the foggy face. And instantly, as if Miles's hands were pushing clouds from the sun, the man's face came into focus.

*"Uncle Aaron?"*

"Miles," Aaron whimpered.

Before Miles could say anything else, Aaron's cheeks sank, and his nose narrowed into a blade of skin and cartilage. The patch of hair on his chin grew long and white. There were burn marks on his face that began to wrinkle and crack like dry clay.

Miles jumped back, not sure of what his uncle was doing there. Who he was turning into. *What* he was turning into.

"Miles," Aaron whispered. Then a little louder. "Miles."

Miles shook his head, looked away, squeezed his eyes shut. Then he opened them and turned back toward Uncle Aaron, whose mouth, slightly opened, now housed rotten teeth.

"Miles," he called again, his voice thickening, Miles's name like slime in his throat. Miles leaned in. Uncle Aaron flashed a sly smile, yanked his now-knobby white hands from the web and wrapped his fingers around Miles's throat, squeezing as hard as he could. *"MILES!"*

The loss of breath.

The kind that comes from falling.

Miles crashed hard onto his twin bed.

"MILES!" Ganke yelled. He was standing in front of Miles's bed in sweatpants and a T-shirt with I LIKE TO MOVE IT, MOVE IT! printed across the front in neon green.

"Huh? Wha—? What's . . . ?" Miles put his hands over his face. "What time is it?"

"Almost seven."

"Ugh." He spread his fingers and peeked through them like fence pickets. "Did I do it again?"

"Yeah, man," Ganke said. "I got up to go to the bathroom and you were literally crawling on the ceiling. And I just gotta tell you, as your friend, it's not cool to wake up to a human-size spider above your head."

"Sorry, man. Just . . . crazy dream."

"Your uncle again?" Ganke asked, sitting back on his bed.

"Yeah," Miles huffed. It wasn't a hard guess for Ganke. Miles had been dreaming about his uncle for a long time. Since he'd watched him die.

That day at the Baruch Houses, Uncle Aaron knew that the spider that bit Miles wasn't just a normal spider. And Miles knew it, too, after watching his uncle step on it and noticing the blood smear radiated on the hardwood. Miles was certain that, even though his uncle didn't intentionally plant the spider, it was obviously *special*, which meant the bite was *special*, which meant there was a good chance Miles would also now be *special*. No longer a regular boy.

"This will be a simple conversation—a short one," Uncle Aaron said the next time they met up as they sat on the couch. No pizza this time. Aaron looked Miles square in the face. "I'll tell people."

"Tell people what?" Miles asked, perplexed.

"About you. About . . . what you can do. What you are." Aaron pointed to the small circular scar on the top of Miles's hand, no bigger than a pimple, then sat back and smiled. He wasn't stupid, he explained to Miles, and he was willing to leak Miles's secret. "Unless . . ."

"Unless what?"

Unless Miles agreed to help him take down a mob boss and former friend of Aaron's everyone called the Scorpion. Miles didn't have a choice. He did what he had to do, and used the fact that the Scorpion was a terrible criminal to justify it. But the threat of ratting Miles out didn't go away. Instead Uncle Aaron demanded that Miles continue to work with him. *For* him. But Miles knew that wasn't an option. When he confronted Aaron, a brutal battle ensued. Aaron got the best of Miles, who was still just a novice at using his powers, leaving nothing but the final blow of one of Aaron's electric gloves, called gauntlets. But the gauntlet malfunctioned and blew up in Aaron's face, leaving him crushed by an explosion he'd planned to use, in a desperate fit, to kill Miles.

"You're just . . . like me," Aaron said, burned and bloody, before losing consciousness. It was the last thing he said to Miles.

When you fight your uncle to the death, it's hard to shake it. Hard to not see his face, his eyes glossing over, his breath slowing, gurgling, stopping. It's hard to keep it a secret. A secret that seems to seep into everything—your immediate family, your school, your sleep. Ganke knew, because Ganke knew everything, but that didn't stop the constant loop playing over and over again in Miles's head.

He could never go back to bed after the nightmares. He tried time and time again, but it was impossible. Plus his alarm was going to go off in a few minutes anyway. So with a disgruntled sigh, Miles got up.

Ganke was in the shower already, and as Miles ventured down the hall of feet funk, sliding lazily in his flip-flops into the bathroom, he could hear Ganke speaking softly to himself in one of the shower stalls. As opposed to the stench of toxic toes in the hallway, the bathroom smelled more like wet dog and corn chips. Steam wafted through the air.

"Who you talking to, Ganke?" Miles groused, turning the knob on the sink faucet. Then catching himself, he added, "You know what? Don't tell me. I don't wanna know."

"Whatever, man. I'm working on my poetry. All three lines have to be between fourteen and sixteen syllables," Ganke explained through the vinyl shower curtain. "So you gotta count 'em out."

Miles cupped his hands under the spigot and splashed water on his face. "Why?" he asked.

"What you mean, *why*?" Ganke snatched one side of the curtain back, just enough to push his face through. "Because my people said so." Then he snatched the curtain closed again, and yelled, *"SIJO!"*

Miles and Ganke flip-flopped back to their room, got dressed—hair-brushing, sneaker-brushing—split a pack of cold Pop-Tarts, and headed out to class. But before they left their dorm, Miles doubled back. Just for a moment. He walked over to the closet and opened the door, Ganke still in the hallway waiting for him. He peered into the pile of clothes and shoes. There in the dark corner was the red-and-black skin he usually carried with him every day, now balled up underneath a mess of BVA sweatshirts, unmatched socks, and spotless sneakers. He stared at it for a few seconds before reaching through the junk and yanking out the mask. He held it up, limp like a melted face, then, shaking his head, stuffed it back down into the pile of leather and laces. *Not today.*

At Brooklyn Visions Academy students only had four classes a semester, but those classes were ninety minutes long. So if you had bad classes, they were extra bad. But at least Miles got to start the day with math.

Calculus, one of Miles's favorite classes, was taught by Mr. Borem, a skeletal man with olive skin and a nose like an ice pick. "Calculus," Mr. Borem had said on the first day of class, jacking his pants up to his navel while pacing across the room, "is the mathematical study of change." But after that speech came the real glory of math, at least to Miles—numbers and symbols and letters. The sweet sight of *one plus one equals alphabet*. A challenge that Miles was always excited about facing.

After that—chemistry with Mrs. Khalil.

Then, while half the students had first lunch, Miles and Ganke headed to Ms. Blaufuss's class.

The thing about Ms. Blaufuss was that she didn't really look like she was supposed to be teaching at BVA. Where was the blazer? The over-starched button-up? The khakis? The "sensible" shoes? She did have the glasses, though, but they weren't the Brooklyn Visions Academy glasses— the wire circles or the plastic rectangles. No, Ms. Blaufuss wore cat-eye frames, bright yellow as if they were made of lemon rinds. Her hair, a choppy short cut, was always tousled. Sometimes she wore dresses, but usually she wore jeans rolled at the ankles, loose blouses, long sweaters scrunched to her elbows, high heels Monday through Thursday, and sneakers on Friday. She had a tattoo on her wrist of a semicolon, and one on her forearm of a slice of pepperoni pizza.

"Mr. Morales, welcome back," she said, as Miles and Ganke entered the classroom. Her room was covered in posters of writers, most of whom Miles had never heard of before. He took his seat. Ganke sat behind him. Winnie Stockton, a *sko-low*—which was what the kids on scholarship called themselves—from Washington Heights, sat in front of him.

"Hi, Ms. Blaufuss," Miles said, a slight twinge of embarrassment in his voice. He knew everyone knew he had been suspended, and more importantly he knew everyone *thought* they knew why. *The kid who had to pee so bad he was willing to be punished for it.* When really he was *the kid who is Spider-Man.* Well, as of the night before, *the kid formerly known as Spider-Man.*

"Yo, Ms. Blaufuss." Ganke followed up, excitedly, "I've been working on my sijos."

"Yeah, he has." Miles shook his head, but stopped shaking it when Alicia Carson sat down at the desk beside him.

Alicia. A beautiful lump in his throat. All brains, brown skin, and braids. A slightly crooked smile and just enough of a lisp to be charming. She smelled like vanilla, but Miles knew there was also a touch of sandalwood, probably a spritz of some kind of perfume just behind her ear. His mother loved sandalwood. Burned sandalwood incense to kill the smell of fried fish in the house all the time.

"Hey, Miles," Alicia said.

"Hey, Alicia." In the corner of his eye, Miles saw Ganke bouncing his eyebrows like a creep. Miles talked to Ganke about Alicia all the time, and, being the best friend he was, Ganke was always trying to convince Miles that she liked him back and that he should make a move. But Miles wouldn't. He couldn't. He wanted to, but all the cool he thought he had was currently balled up into a spandex mess in his closet.

"Okay, everyone, settle down." Ms. Blaufuss stood in the front of the class with just her fingers tucked into her jean pockets. "I hope everybody had a good weekend. I hope you all took a moment to breathe in the poetry all around you." *The poetry all around you.* Normally statements like that made Miles cringe, but Ms. Blaufuss could get away with it. "We're going to be working on sijos all week, using the first ten minutes of class to write. It doesn't have to be perfect or even finished, but I want you to build your syllabic muscles." Ms. Blaufuss curled her arm as if flexing her bicep. "Now, does anybody wanna throw out a prompt we should use?" Chrissy Bentley, who was sitting on the other side of the room, flung her hand up. "Chrissy?"

"Dogs."

"*Dogs?*" Ryan Ratcliffe scowled.

"Yeah, what's wrong with dogs?"

Ganke leaned forward and whispered in Miles's ear, "Dude, I can't write a sijo about a cockapoo. Not gonna do it." Miles held in his laughter.

"Okay, so Ryan, what do you think is a better prompt?" Ms. Blaufuss asked.

"I mean . . ." Ryan wiped one hand over the other as if he were washing them. "Love."

The class groaned. *Seriously?* Ryan "Ratshit" Ratcliffe was the kind of dude who never left his dorm without splashing his neck in old-man cologne that smelled like black pepper. Plus he had the *I look like I might be on TV* thing down. Blue eyes. Face like it had been chiseled out of stone. Teeth like they'd been specially made from elephant tusk. Dude was *so* TV. *So* gross.

"Love, huh?" Ms. Blaufuss said. "Okay, well, how 'bout we do love, but we keep it open. That way, Chrissy, you can talk about how much you love your dog. Ryan, you can talk about how much you love—"

"Yourself," Chrissy dropped in. The class rumbled with muted laughter. Ryan was too cool to even be fazed.

"Or whatever you want." Ms. Blaufuss pinched back a chuckle. "Everyone can use the *love* prompt any way they desire, okay? Ten minutes, starting . . . now."

The class instantly quieted. Ms. Blaufuss darted over to Miles and squatted beside his desk.

"Has Ganke explained any of this to you?" she whispered.

"He . . . sorta."

"I tried," Ganke said, too loud.

"*Shhhh,*" from someone in the class.

"He tried," Miles confirmed.

"Okay, it's real simple. Three lines. Each one has to be between fourteen and sixteen syllables. And they all have jobs. The first line sets up the situation, the second develops it, and the third is the twist." Ms. Blaufuss spun the top off of an invisible bottle. "Got it?"

Seemed easy enough. But once Miles started thinking about what he wanted to write about, especially as it pertained to love, he got stuck. Of course, there was his mother—she was the easiest person to write about, but he didn't know what to say about her. *I love you* is only three syllables. *I love you, Ma*—four. *I love you so much, Ma*—six. Or he could write about his father. Miles had been thinking about him a lot since he got back to BVA the night before. Thinking about the talk on the stoop about how Uncle Aaron had been suspended a lot. About how the most heroic thing you could do is take care of your community. About how sometimes to love someone, you have to be hard on them. Miles started scribbling.

*My father's love looks like . . .*

Miles counted out the syllables on his fingers. Started again.

*To my father, love sometimes means—*

"And *time's up*," Ms. Blaufuss announced. *Ugh*. He was just finding his groove. "Does anyone want to share?" Ms. Blaufuss asked.

Lots of hands went up, and Miles didn't have to turn around to know that Ganke was waving his around like a madman.

"Um . . . how 'bout . . . you, Alicia." Ms. Blaufuss motioned for her, smiling. Miles could hear Ganke deflating behind him, his frustrated breath crawling up the back of Miles's neck. "Come up to the front of the class." Alicia took her place in front of everyone, her paper in her hand, the purple ink bleeding through the back. "What's the name of your sijo?"

"It's untitled," Alicia said. She pursed her lips for just a second, then began.

"A romantic mountaintop view of the world is love
    for most
Being that close to clouds strips them of form, turns
    them to fog
Perhaps the real beauty is on the way up, where *like* is."

The class erupted for a grinning Alicia as she returned to her seat.

"That was amazing," Miles leaned over and said to her. She was known around BVA as a poet and even headed up the school's poetry club—the Dream Defenders—which of course, Ms. Blaufuss was the advisor of. Miles figured she was good—he never thought anything negative about her, ever—but he had never actually been to any of the poetry club's events, mainly because he didn't think he'd get it. Only one person could say stuff like *the poetry all around you*, and that person was not a teenager. Unless of course, Alicia said it. She could've said anything. She could've written about her love for freakin' . . . cockapoos, and Miles would've found some redeeming quality in it.

"Thanks," she said, blushing slightly.

"Fantastic, Alicia," Ms. Blaufuss said. "I should mention, Alicia and the Dream Defenders will be hosting an open mic this evening at six in the quad. I'd love to see you all there sharing some of this work, okay? And to sweeten the pot, if you show up, there's extra credit in it for you. Poetry is about community—it's not just about expression, but also being a witness to that expression." Ms. Blaufuss glanced at Miles. He could definitely use the extra credit. "Again, nice job, Alicia."

"Yo, you think maybe Alicia's half-Korean?" Ganke whispered in Miles's ear.

Miles didn't respond. Just swatted Ganke's words away like a swarm of annoying gnats.

In the midst of the cafeteria cacophony of pitchy voices, Miles choked down what he could of his lunch and took two small sips of apple juice before the bell rang. Kids jumped up from the lunch tables and poured into the hall. Ganke, who had already had Chamberlain's class that morning, slapped Miles's hand before they went their separate ways.

"Good luck," Ganke said.

"Yeah, thanks."

Cue the ominous organ music.

As Miles entered the classroom, Mr. Chamberlain was scribbling a quote passionately across the board, his handwriting scratchy and jagged. When he finished writing, Mr. Chamberlain turned to face the students, still filling in their desks. His skin was yellowy and thin, and his lips—beneath his furry slug of a mustache—were chapped from constant licking. He assumed his normal meditative stance—hands together, woven fingers, his face a tight fist.

"War means fighting, and fighting means killing," he said softly. Miles refused to look him in the face. Actually he refused to look anyone in the face, still embarrassed about how the suspension went down. Alicia, who also had this class with Miles, sat in front of him. *Right* in front of him.

"War means fighting, and fighting means killing," Mr. Chamberlain repeated, the students settling into silence.

He was referring to the quote he'd scrawled on the board behind him. "War . . ." he started again, now closing his eyes. There was a hush in the room. For a few, it was because they were amused. For others, like Miles, it was out of respect . . . or maybe fear. But for most, it was from boredom. Most students used Mr. Chamberlain's class as nap time, dozing off while he droned from the front of the room with closed eyes, almost as if he was speaking in some kind of intense dream state. "War means fighting, and fighting means killing," he repeated for the last time. Every day, he delivered a new quote three times like a chant, an incantation summoning the spirit of *this sucks*.

And . . . this sucked.

Mr. Chamberlain picked up right where Ganke said he left off, explaining to the class what America would be if slavery hadn't existed.

"It could be argued that the country as we know it wouldn't even be here. The luxuries you all love so much, like your precious cell phones, might still be just a lofty thought meant for an alien planet somewhere far away. Slavery was the building block of our great country. We shouldn't just blindly write off the argument for the Confederacy wanting to keep it. It could very well be argued that they weren't just fighting for the present, but also for the future."

While Mr. Chamberlain was yapping, Miles squirmed in his seat. Not because he had to go to the bathroom— no, he knew what Mr. Chamberlain was stating so boldly was dead wrong. Morally. There were so many things to consider. The most obvious was . . . *slavery*. Human beings enslaved, mistreated, killed.

Then again, maybe Chamberlain was calling everyone's bluff—all the bored students who he had to know weren't paying any attention. Maybe he was trying to make them angry so they would engage. Like Brad Canby, a trust-fund goon with a pockmarked face who was always more concerned with getting a laugh than getting an A. He never paid attention in any class, but especially not in Mr. Chamberlain's. But judging from Alicia's head shaking in front of him, Miles knew she was just as disturbed by what the teacher was saying. And that was enough to make him put his hand up.

But before he could call out for Mr. Chamberlain—who could never see raised hands because his eyes were always closed—Miles lowered his hand. Then he brought it up to his temple.

His head was buzzing.

*Oh no. Not again.*

Miles sat still in his desk, trying to block Mr. Chamberlain out and let it pass. *The buzzing will go away. No big deal. It's nothing, anyway.* But Mr. Chamberlain was really digging in now. "And, though given so much credit after the war for freeing slaves, it mustn't be ignored that at the beginning of his presidency, Abraham Lincoln's policies shifted dramatically from the antislavery platform he'd campaigned on."

*Buzz. Buzz.*

Mr. Chamberlain's voice distorted in Miles's ears. *Don't*

*get up. It'll pass. It's nothing. It's probably nothing.* He stared at the back of Alicia's neck, the fuzzy hair left unbraided at her nape, curling toward him. *What if . . . ? No. But seriously, what if someone's hurt? What if the city's being torn apart?* He kept trying to ignore it, but with every pulsing vibration came the nagging possibility that someone was in danger.

Miles Morales was having a full-on meltdown.

Miles thought about the people he saw in his neighborhood tweaking on the block, trying to fight off whatever they might've been addicted to. The old men, crashing into the bodega door with the shakes, just trying to get to the fridge. The ladies, scratching their heads and forearms, trying to remember how to get home. Trying to remember when they left the house in the first place. The Cyrus Shines.

"They going through it," Miles's father would say to explain the withdrawal, the sickness. "Hang in there," he'd say to them as he and Miles walked by.

Miles needed to hang in there. To resist the urge to save someone other than himself. But he was getting lightheaded. His heart was beating faster than it ever had, and it felt like his veins had tightened, making it possible to actually *feel* the blood coursing through his body.

To try to steady his mind, he fell into a routine, a pattern to get through the class.

*Buzz. Buzz. Buzz. Buzz.*

*Breathe. Blink the blur away. Breathe.*

*Sandalwood. Calm.*

*Buzz. Buzz. Buzz. Buzz.*

*Block out the droning wah-wah-wah of Mr. Chamberlain's voice.*

"Yes, the Thirteenth Amendment states that there shall be no more slavery in the United States, except as punishment for crime. Perhaps it could be argued that the enslavement of our criminals is still keeping our great country alive." That statement was like a needle stuck in Miles's spine, tightening his body, forcing him to glance up. He caught Chamberlain's eyes, which, surprisingly, were open just for a moment, leering directly at him. Then Chamberlain closed his eyes, steeled his face, and finished his statement. "That is, in the minds of our Confederate forefathers."

*Buzz.*

*Breathe. Blink the blur away. Breathe.*

*Was he . . . smiling?*

*Sandalwood. Calm.*

Alicia, sensing Miles staring at the back of her neck like a weirdo, turned to the side, caught him out of the corner of her eye. Smirked, her cheek dimpling deep enough for Miles to want to dive in.

*Sandalwood. Calm. Breathe. Breathe.*

And then, finally . . . *finally* . . . the bell rang. Chair legs scraped against linoleum as people jumped up from their desks. Miles slowly stood, a ring of sweat around his T-shirt collar, relieved. He'd made it.

"You think he's serious, or is he baiting us?" Alicia spoke softly to Miles as she packed her books away in her bag.

"Um . . . I don't know," Miles said, wiping his forehead, then zipping his bag. Mr. Chamberlain was erasing the quote he'd written at the beginning of class. Miles scowled at his back.

"Why you looking like that?" Alicia uttered, studying Miles's face. Miles caught himself and turned his grimace to a grin. But Alicia seemed doubly confused. "Now, why you looking like *that*? Did you *enjoy* that mess?"

"What, the class?" Miles looked down for a moment to gather himself. "Of course not. No. *No*." His head still buzzing, his stomach still churning, sweat still leaking from his skin. He probably looked like he had pneumonia. *Don't pass out,* he thought. *Don't pass out.* And while coaching himself out of passing out, he also knew he couldn't pass up on this opportunity to say something nice about Alicia. A compliment. But not about the way she looked or smelled or the slight *th* she substituted for every *s*. He needed to say something that would offset the creepy look on his face. Then it hit him—he'd tell her how much he'd liked her poem. About the mountain. Of love. And like. "Hey . . . um . . . so, this is random but I enjoyed your po—" he started, but the words got trapped under the rock rolling up his throat. He swallowed it back down, and tried again, no longer smiling. A burp escaped. Alicia cocked her head to the side. "Sorry." Miles covered his mouth to block belch breath. "I was saying I—" His words

caught again. "I was saying I enjoyed your . . . your . . ."
Suddenly it was more than just hiccups or burps. He was
heaving. Alicia took a step back, stared at him, a look of
concern on her face.

"Miles?"

"Sorry, sorry, I . . ." He put a hand over his mouth,
lurched forward. "Oh . . . God. I . . ." And then he bolted
away from Alicia, past Mr. Chamberlain, almost bowling
over the lingering students standing in the doorway, to get
to the bathroom.

*Buzz.*

*Buzz.*

*Buzz.*

## CHAPTER FIVE

"**Y**ooooo." Ganke came slamming into the dorm room, holding some envelopes in one hand, and waving around an orange piece of paper in the other. Miles was lying on his side scribbling his best version of a sijo. He glanced up at Ganke. Ganke slowed. "What's wrong with you?"

Miles put his pen down. "I talked to Alicia. Like, *talked to her* talked to her."

"Okay, and . . ."

"And . . . I almost threw up on her."

"Wait. You mean, like, you actually almost puked on her? Like . . . puked pesto penne pas—"

"Yes, man," Miles cut him off. Ganke strained his neck muscles to stifle his smile, but couldn't hold it. He threw the envelopes on his desk and slapped his hand over his mouth to muzzle the laughter. "It's *not* funny," Miles grumped.

"Oh, I know it's not. I mean, it is. But it's also not. Because it's . . . *disgusting*. Like, there's not enough hot water on Earth to make you ever feel clean again. I mean, I would have to figure out if there's some kind of surgery to replace my skin if somebody splashed me with a vomit comet." He mimed a gag. "Seriously, think about—"

"Yo, you wanna hear what happened or not?"

"Yeah, yeah. Sorry."

Miles ran through the story—Chamberlain's lesson, the spidey-sense malfunction, the small talk with Alicia, and of course, the almost-upchuck, which led to a mad dash down the hall to the boys' bathroom.

"But by the time I made it into a stall, the feeling was gone. My spidey-sense had finally worn off, or . . . whatever."

"What?"

"Nothing, I just . . . I don't know." Miles scratched his chin. "Chamberlain gave me this look."

"What kind of look?"

"Like, a look. I can't explain it." Miles took a second to think about that moment in class. The way he was feeling, Chamberlain's searing eyes. "I mean, you know how every time my spidey-sense starts buggin' out and I run to see what's going on and I never find anything?" Ganke nodded, and Miles continued. "Well, what if it's coming from *inside* the classroom?"

"You mean . . ."

"I mean, what if it's him setting it off?"

Ganke looked at Miles sideways, then closed his eyes and shook his head in disbelief. "Look, Chamberlain's *definitely* out of his mind. Like . . . out there. The mess he says in class proves that for sure. Plus, you *know* he probably eats stuff like cottage cheese, and anybody who eats that crap gotta be evil, not just to people around them, but also to their own taste buds and butts, because I hear cottage cheese makes you—"

"Ganke." Miles put his hand up, waving the rest of that sentence off. Nobody wanted to think about Mr. Chamberlain that way.

"I'm just saying, I love you, but, bro, you're reaching. And I get it. You need an excuse to get over the fact that you just blew it with Alicia."

Miles pushed a gust of air from his nostrils, slapped his hands to his face and massaged his brow line. "I guess. Maybe you're right."

"*Except* . . . maybe not." Ganke floated the orange paper over to Miles's bed. "At least not about the Alicia thing."

Ganke nodded mischievously as Miles grabbed the paper and held it up to his face.

THE BVA SENIOR CLASS, IN CONJUNCTION
WITH THE HISTORY DEPARTMENT, PRESENTS:
THE SCHOOL GHOUL FEST

Miles slapped the paper down. "Ganke, we never go to this."

"I *know*. Just figured it was worth a shot since you keep acting like your Super Hero days are over. Since you've decided people don't need saving no more. And I feel you, why should you be responsible for looking out for so many strangers *just* because you have superhuman strength?" Ganke dramatically turned away.

"I know what you're trying to do."

"Come on," Ganke pleaded, now turning back to Miles. "The city *needs* you, especially on Halloween. And even though this might be an opportunity to try to fix it with Alicia"—he pointed to the paper—"*this* is who you are. What you do." Ganke put his arms out, palms up, and pretended to shoot some web. "You're Spider-Man, whether you like it or not."

"Ganke . . . don't." Miles's tone shifted. He reached over and grabbed the invitation, skimmed the details. Judge, a sko-low who grew up in Flatbush, was deejaying. If he was controlling the music, it was guaranteed the party was going to be live. Miles studied the invitation again, as if it were some kind of code to cool. Or girls. Or cool girls. Like Alicia. Or . . . just a damn good time as Miles Morales. *Not* Spider-Man.

After a few moments, he lay flat on his back, the party invitation slipping from the mattress and sailing down to the floor. He'd always heard great things about the Halloween party. And Ganke was right, they'd missed it their freshman and sophomore years and, afterward, were forced to stomach the weeklong social media exhibition of selfies and group shots. Not to mention everyone talking about the yearly Halloween prank. *Ugh.* Miles always acted like it didn't bother him. That he was unfazed by the fun on everyone's faces. But the truth was, it got to him. A little.

But Ganke didn't press the issue, not about the party or Miles's "retirement." Just let it rest until out of the blue, Miles's alarm clock went off. Ganke flinched.

"Dude, you're already awake." At this point, Ganke had pulled a thick textbook from his bag and set it on his lap. He had also kicked off his shoes and was smelling the insides. *Seriously, why?*

"I know, but I set it just in case I fell asleep so I wouldn't be late for work. Which, by the way, I wish I didn't have to go to, because I'd rather be at the poetry event." Miles couldn't believe he'd just said that, but he needed more than just redemption with Alicia—he needed the extra credit. Miles sat back up, swiped both hands down his face as if he were wiping the tired off, then grabbed the notebook with his failed sijo attempts from the corner of his bed. "How am I supposed to work to keep some of the weight off my folks, *and* do stuff like extra credit? It's hard to do extra anything, y'know?" Then, after a pregnant pause, Miles simply asked, "If I don't go to this party, would you go without me?"

"Depends. Are you not going because you have to watch over the city dressed in tights and a mask?"

"No."

"Then, yes."

Miles *hmph*'d and glanced down at the invitation on the

floor, a corny graphic of blood dripping and ghost em
above the text.

"Okay." He randomly lobbed the word in the air as if it were obvious what it was connected to.

"Okay . . . what?" Ganke was clearly confused.

"Okay, I'm in." Miles sighed.

"In . . . ?"

"Come on, Ganke. You know what I'm talking about."

"The Halloween party?" His mouth twisted into an uncertain frown. "You sure you don't think you should, you know . . ." Ganke did the awful web-shooting impression again.

"I just need to . . . not . . . be . . . all that," Miles said awkwardly. "Look, we goin' or not?"

And just like that, it was settled.

While Ganke, now bubbling with excitement, blabbered on about ideas for costumes, Miles got dressed for work. As he zipped up his backpack and wiggled his feet into his sneakers, he asked Ganke as casually as possible, "By the way, what about you? You going to the poetry club event?"

"Not sure yet. I mean, I want to because, you know . . . I got heat. But I also got chem homework." He tapped the book he had resting on his lap. "Nothing like a little chemical bonding to round out the night."

"I wish," Miles replied, smirking. "Well, if for some reason you end up there, can you just apologize to Alicia for me?" Miles tossed his notebook in his bag and slung it over his shoulder. He headed toward the door, but stopped and flipped through their mail. There was

s name on it. Miles slipped it into his back

, I got you." Ganke thumbed up. "If I go, I'll tell her.

"Thanks, man."

And as Miles pushed the door closed behind him, Ganke yelled, "That you *love* her!"

Campus Convenience: The store that's sure to bore. Miles's job was part of the work-study program, and it was basically a way for him to get free room and board so that his parents could keep a roof over their own heads. Rent in their neighborhood was going up yearly, and there was always the fear that their landlord—a man named Caesar that no one ever saw—would sell it, which would leave Miles and his parents scrambling for housing. Miles had seen it happen before. A man named Mr. Oscar used to live at the end of the block. Been there Miles's whole life. Until a FOR SALE sign went up beside his stoop. Until people started standing around outside, looking up at the windows, scribbling in notepads, typing on cell phones. Until Mr. Oscar wasn't there anymore.

Whenever Miles thought about this, he pictured his mother and father crammed up in the dorm with him and Ganke, his mother trying to microwave plátanos on Sundays. Miles, sleeping head-to-toe in Ganke's bed, while some new family moved into his home. A family like Brad

Canby's or Ryan Ratcliffe's. A family that ate off good china every night.

It was a ridiculous image. But it was enough motivation to keep Miles going to work.

But the thing about Campus Convenience is that it *conveniently* didn't sell anything any actual teenagers wanted. No phone chargers, no nail polish. Just notebooks, tear-off or spiral. Pens, felt-tip or ballpoint. Pencils, no. 2 or mechanical. And of course, sausage in a can. And Miles's job was to ring up the teachers and students who would pop in to buy something. Which meant Miles's job was to do nothing. Because no one wanted sausage in a can.

Miles stood hunched over the counter, his life raft in a sea of one-ply toilet paper and three-hole punchers. There was nothing to do, no one to talk to, and what made it worse was the music—saxophones crooning a perfect soundtrack to a workplace wasteland.

So Miles did what he always did at work: homework. He'd finished his chemistry and breezed through his calculus before leaving the dorm. And no history assignment, as usual. Mr. Chamberlain made it so that the entire grade was based on tests. No extra credit. No special assignments. Just listen and . . . regurgitate.

So it was just Miles and the sijo. The prompt, a piece of cake and a knife in the gut at the same time: write about family. It had been giving him trouble since he'd started it, hours before. But before he could, again, try to tap into his inner Edgar Allan Poe, he remembered the envelope in his back pocket. He pulled it out and glanced at the return address he hadn't bothered to look at on his way out the door.

Austin Davis
7000 Old Factory Road
Brooklyn, NY 11209

Miles Morales
Brooklyn Visions Academy
Patterson Hall RM 352
Brooklyn, New York, 11229

Miles slipped his thumb along the closure and slowly tore the envelope open. Slipped the letter out, unfolded it, revealing line after line of penciled words, written in all capital letters.

MILES,
IF YOU'RE READING THIS, THAT MEANS MY
GRANDMA REALLY DOES KNOW HOW TO
USE THE INTERNET. SHE TOLD ME SHE WAS
GOING TO SEARCH FOR YOU. AND NOW
YOU'RE PROBABLY WONDERING WHO I AM
AND WHAT THIS LETTER IS ABOUT. MY NAME
IS AUSTIN. MY FATHER'S NAME WAS AARON
DAVIS. IF GRANDMA IS RIGHT, AARON DAVIS
WAS YOUR UNCLE, WHICH MAKES ME YOUR
COUSIN.

Miles's eyes scanned *which makes me your cousin* over and over again, mainly because he didn't know his uncle had any children, and also because he didn't have any other cousins. *Which makes me your cousin.* Uncle Aaron had a son? *Which makes me your cousin.* Miles kept reading, other words jumping off the page like *fifteen* and *locked up* and *if you write back.*

*Locked up.*

*Cousin.*

*Austin.*

And when Miles reached the end of the letter, he started over, and read the whole thing again. His saliva turned sour, a syrup oozing slowly down his throat. He didn't know what to think, if he should even believe what he was reading. He couldn't. This couldn't be true. How could Uncle Aaron have a kid and Miles not know about it? Did his father know? He had to. But maybe not, because he and Aaron never spoke. But still . . . he had to. Besides, Miles talked to Aaron all the time. Well, he used to, before . . . before. Wouldn't Aaron have said something? Wouldn't there have been something to give it away? A picture? Something?

A loud thump snapped Miles out of his haze. A group of obnoxious students walking by the store had banged on the window. Miles instinctively folded the letter as if he had been caught doing something wrong. But once he set his eyes on the fools in the BVA it-crowd, he relaxed. Didn't really seem like the poetry types, but he assumed they were heading to the quad for the event anyway—everybody loved Alicia and her crew. He figured at least one of them would pop into the store, maybe for candy, water, sausage in a can, a stupid joke, a random rich-kid taunt which typically sounded like gold-plated fart noises . . . anything to shake up the boredom. But nope. They kept walking, leaving Miles with his thoughts, with the contents of the letter, with the idea of Austin—and Aaron—all dancing off beat through his mind to the sound of smooth jazz.

He unfolded the letter again. It had been folded in thirds to fit into the envelope, and it was obvious that Austin had struggled to get it right from the different creases making veins across the paper. As soon as the letter was open again, there was another bang on the glass. But this time it was Ganke. His face was contorted against the window, as if he'd had a run-in with the crew that had just walked by. He kept his face mashed on the glass, his lips sliming up into a smile as if they were made of lava. Then he unstuck himself and yanked the door open.

"Sorry to interrupt. I know this is the busiest time of your shift," Ganke said, standing in front of the counter with his arms spread, turning in circles.

"Shut up." Miles folded the letter again. "Ain't you supposed to be doing homework?"

"Yeah, well. I got most of the chemistry done and started working on my sijo. But the prompt is . . . I don't know . . . kinda got me stuck."

"Family?"

"Yeah, man." Ganke's voice slipped from silly to serious. "Like, what am I supposed to write? My-fah-ther-and-muh-ther-have-bro-ken-up-and-I-am-sad?" Ganke counted on his fingers. "This is a true statement, but not exactly my best work."

"I feel you. I was working on it earlier, and was struggling, but after reading this, it seems even more impossible." Miles extended Austin's letter to Ganke.

Ganke took the letter, unfolded it, and began reading. His eyes darted across the page, spreading wider with each word. "Who . . . ?" Ganke glanced up from the page. "Who is this from?"

"You read it. Apparently my uncle had a son. Named Austin. Who's fifteen. And in jail." All fact, no feeling.

"Whoa." Ganke refolded the letter and handed it back to Miles. "You gon' tell your father?"

"I don't know," Miles said, sliding the letter back into the envelope. He folded it in half and slipped it into the small pouch in the front of his backpack. When he lifted his eyes back to Ganke, a look of stress had smeared across his face. He shook his head. "Anyway, what you come here for? You need something?"

"Do I need something? Really, Miles?" Ganke teased, each word soaked in sarcasm. "I actually came to tell you that I was going to the open mic. I'm hoping the extra credit will offset me not getting my sijo done, in case the family thing, y'know, stumps me." A flash of pain struck Ganke's face, but it left as quickly as it came. "*And* I wanted to make sure you knew I was also gonna put in a word for you. Get it? Put in a *word* for you? A *word*? With Alicia? At the poetry open mic? *Word?*"

"I get it."

"Got it."

"Please leave."

"I'll take that as a thank-you. And you're welcome." Ganke threw the words at Miles like a no-look pass as he left the store.

Leaving Miles alone.

Miles leaned onto the counter, using his elbows to prop himself up, still trying to wrap his mind around the whole Austin thing. He wondered if he should tell his father. Or if he should write back. Or maybe just ignore it. Besides, how could he prove it was true, that this was his actual cousin? He could go see him. That was an option. But not really. That *wasn't* an option. He'd need one of his parents to take him to the jail, and telling his father—though another option—wasn't really a good one either. His father wanted nothing to do with Aaron and insisted Miles also have nothing to do with Aaron, so there was a good chance Miles's dad would want that embargo to remain intact. But Miles couldn't help but think about it. About what Austin looked like. About how he ended up behind bars. About what Austin knew of his father's death.

Guilt crashed into him, shaking every bone in his body as a saxophone solo blared through the speakers. But there was nothing to do, nowhere to put the guilt except—and he couldn't believe he was even thinking this—his homework.

The poetry assignment. For once, the store being empty and boring seemed like a good thing.

Miles yanked his notebook from his backpack, flipped it open, stared at what he had already written in the dorm. Then ripped that out, crumpled it into a ball, and did a stiff hook shot to the garbage can. Missed. Basketball just wasn't his sport.

He started again. Actually, he stared at the paper and thought about starting again, waiting for the words in his head to somehow pop onto the page. He hadn't even pulled out a pen yet.

*Austin. Aaron. Dad.*

Family. That was Ms. Blaufuss's new prompt. *Write two sijo poems about your family, something you love and something you don't.* Miles kept eyeing the page, the saxophone crooning, making it hard for him to think about a family whose soundtrack wouldn't be anything as soft as this.

Finally, he reached in his bag for a pen.

~~WHAT I LOVE~~
WHAT I HATE
~~smooth jazz~~
I hate my father's face when he tells me my block is my
    burden
like my job is to carry a family I didn't create
~~to somehow erase the blood he left in the street like~~
    ~~cursive~~
like my life is for fixing something I didn't even break

79

WHAT I LOVE
The way my mother says, "Mijo. Sunday dinner is
    ready"
and kisses my father gently while I set the table
~~If only we were more like her~~
~~If only everyone were as gentle and loving~~
The way she looks at us like we're perfect, though
    we're not


Miles scribbled and scratched out, scribbled and scratched out, over and over again trying to find the right words, the right count. And what he landed on, what he finally came up with, he hated. *Ugh.* A poet would have a better grasp on language. A better understanding of how to put words together to at least communicate a coherent idea. *Exhibit A: Austin, if we are in fact family, I wish I would've known you a long time ago. Being an only child means you fight every battle alone. Plus, I always wanted bunk beds.* Or *Exhibit B: Alicia, I like you. I like the way you think, the way you look, the way the hair curls on the back of your neck, and I'd like to invite you to split an order of chicken fingers in the dining hall, as a precursor to my mother's chicharrón de pollo on a Sunday in the near future.* But instead, all Miles had was C-grade poetry and a near-puke situation.

More kids walked by. And Miles imagined what else he would say to Alicia if he could just get the courage. It frustrated him that he could wrestle with monsters ten times his size, but not get his mouth to cooperate whenever he was in her presence. So, at the risk of embarrassing himself only in his own mind, he scribbled another sijo, this one not a part of any assignment.

UNTITLED
I'm not even sure that people write love letters
  anymore
and if this is one, I'm sorry for using it to tell you
that I've always known, from the beginning, it's
  sandalwood

Another group—baseball caps, school hoodies—traipsed by. And another. It seemed like the whole school was going to the open mic. Ganke was probably already there. And he'd probably already talked to Alicia for Miles, which should've been a comforting thought. But Miles knew that the likelihood of Ganke just walking up to Alicia and saying *Hey, Alicia, Miles wanted me to tell you that he's sorry about what happened today* was basically at a negative number Mr. Borem had yet to teach.

That, along with the fact that Miles had written what he thought were two terrible poems (though the one about Alicia was decent) and would surely *need* the extra credit, was all he needed to push him over the top. He had to get to the open mic. He had to make sure he was accounted for, and he had to get this poem to Alicia. He could just slip it to her without having to make a big fuss about everything. She could read it when she got back to her room, and tomorrow, they could at least have a human conversation. Maybe. Probably. Hopefully.

But how? How was he going to get out of work? It's not like he could call someone to cover for him. Well, he could, but then he'd have to lie about being sick and all that, and he wasn't up for the theatrics. The only other way he could think of was to just step out for a few minutes, run to the quad, make sure Ms. Blaufuss knew he was there, say what he needed to say to Alicia, and then head back to the store before anyone came in. He'd already been there over an hour without one single customer. Odds were, no one would ever know.

But first, he had to figure out how to deal with the camera.

There was only one security camera and it was just above his head. Miles didn't know if Dean Kushner had anyone check the footage, but he knew there was a good chance no one ever did. It would've been a waste of time to review a store surveillance film of the back of Miles's head every other day, occasionally catching him nodding off. But to be safe, Miles needed to disconnect it, just for the little while he was gone.

Based on what he'd seen in every heist movie he'd watched with his dad, Miles knew one of the most consistent blind spots for any surveillance camera is right underneath it. And if he did this right, the footage would just look like he stepped back for a moment, out of the frame, and then stepped back into it.

Miles backed up as far as he could, until he was just about up against the wall, the camera directly above him. He listened for more bumbling kids. Heard nothing. Then, in a flash, he slipped into camo mode, his entire body, including his clothes, blending in with the eggshell paint. He climbed up the wall until he was eye level with the back of the camera. There was a thick black cord, obviously connecting to the power source. He yanked it out. Then climbed down, coming out of camouflage as if literally stepping out of the wall. He listened again for more students, but heard nothing. Then he ripped the Alicia sijo from his notebook, folded it up, slid it in his pocket, and slipped out the door.

The quad was just a square patch of cement in the middle of campus with benches and a small fountain pool that seniors threw their dorm keys in before graduating. Dean Kushner fined every senior who didn't turn in a key before walking across the stage, but nobody cared about the petty fine—the key tossing was tradition. By the time Miles showed up, the benches were all occupied, girls crammed on each other's laps, guys perched on the corners of the wooden seats. Everyone else stood around the key pool, listening to whoever's turn it was to recite.

Of course, Ryan "Ratshit" Ratcliffe was mid-poem, as Miles ghosted around the perimeter of the crowd.

"I just need you to know that I'll be right here, because I love you today, and I'll love you next year, and I know I seem cold, but that's just 'cause I fear, that you'll break my heart. Don't break my heart. My heart. Don't break it, girl." Ryan's voice had slipped into sexy-poetry tone. As people *kinda* clapped and shook their heads, and Ryan took a bow—of course Ryan took a bow—Alicia emerged from the crowd. Miles couldn't see her at first, just the braided bun on top of her head. But then she stepped up onto the wall of the fountain.

And almost on perfect cue, the buzzing in his head and stomach began.

"Let's give it up for Ryan, y'all!" she said with forced enthusiasm. "Thank you for sharing. Let's see who we have next." While Alicia read down a wrinkled piece of paper containing the list of readers and performers, Miles scanned the room for Ganke, stretching his neck to see if he could catch a glimpse of Ganke's jet-black hair in the sea of blond, brown, and red. He looked to the left. Winnie Stockton, who could only be there because she opted to do her work-study one hour every morning before class, and weekends, standing between Ms. Blaufuss and Mr. Chamberlain. *What was he doing here?* Miles thought at first, but realized that Mr. Chamberlain fit the stereotype of everything Miles hated about poets. Super serious. Hands pressed. Eyes closed. Repeating himself, just for effect. *Ugh.*

Quickly, Miles ran over to Ms. Blaufuss. Because . . . priorities.

"Hey, Ms. Blaufuss."

"Miles!" Ms. Blaufuss lit up when she saw him. "So glad you could make it!"

"Thanks, um, I can only stay for a second because—"
*Buzz. Fight against it. Push it away. You know it's nothing.*

"Because you're supposed to be working, aren't you, Morales?" Mr. Chamberlain interjected. Miles locked eyes with him. And again, there was something there, something behind Mr. Chamberlain's pupils, retracting to let less light in. Something . . . off. Mr. Chamberlain's tone was just sharp enough for Ms. Blaufuss to open her mouth in protest.

"Miles," Ms. Blaufuss said, glaring at Mr. Chamberlain. "Stay as long as you can. I got you marked." She jotted his name in a small notepad. Mr. Chamberlain walked off. Not just to a different part of the crowd, but out of the crowd altogether, as if one stern glare from Ms. Blaufuss was enough to melt his cold, cold heart.

"Thank you," Miles said, unsettled and confused. But he was happy Mr. Chamberlain was gone. Actually, he was happy about that *and* the extra credit. Now with the first note of business complete, it was time to address the second.

He set his sights back on Alicia, who was reading a short poem she said her great-grandmother had written during the Harlem Renaissance. That was the other thing about Alicia that was different. She was Harlem royalty. Old black money. A descendant of artists who hobnobbed with people like Langston Hughes and Jacob Lawrence. As a matter of fact, her family were major donors to BVA, making it possible for kids like Miles and Winnie and Judge to attend.

"My great-granny and her peers were the Dream Defenders of their time. And with that, I'm happy to invite to the mic, as far as I'm concerned, one of the great ones from ours." Miles caught Alicia's eye as she wound up her intro, and an unusual smile crept onto her face. "Put your hands together for my girl, Dawn Leary."

Once Dawn took center stage, Alicia pushed through the crowd toward Miles. He reached in his pocket and pulled out the folded piece of paper—the poem. Her poem. But it just so happened that coming from the other direction—from the other side of the swarm of students—was Ganke.

"Hey, man, you made it!" Ganke said, throwing an arm around Miles. Miles immediately shoved the poem back in his pants.

And before Miles could reply, Alicia called out, "Miles!" and slipped past the last person standing between them. Miles pulled the poem back out. But only halfway. Elbowed Ganke in the ribs as cool as possible, which for Miles was not cool at all.

Ganke grunted. He took his arm from around Miles's shoulder, a smirk dripping off his face. "Um, I . . . will . . . talk . . . to you later," he said robotically, backing away even more awkwardly.

"I swear, Ganke is one of the strangest dudes I know. And I love it." Alicia watched quizzically as Ganke faded back into the crowd.

"Yeah." Miles ignored Ganke's silliness and tried to swallow his nerves as Alicia turned back to him.

"Anyway, it's crazy to see you here." She leaned in for

a hug, as Miles jutted his hand out. Then noticing Alicia was going for the hug, he jutted his other hand out as if he were welcoming a slow dance. But Alicia pulled back, confused but still smiling, and awkwardly extended her hand for a bungled shake. Sandalwood and a hint of sweat rushed Miles's nostrils.

"Why you say that?" Miles said to Alicia way too bluntly. He tried to laugh it off, but that made it even weirder. "I mean . . . I like poetry."

"Is that right? *You* like poetry?" Alicia replied, seeing right through him.

"Yeah. I like yours. And, um, your great-grandmother's." Miles slid the rest of the folded paper from his pocket. "That's art *and* history. Love that."

"Do you? Well, maybe art, but I don't know about history, since it seemed to make you sick earlier today." Her face flowed from excitement to concern. "You good?"

"Oh yeah, that. Yeah . . . I'm fine. Just . . . cafeteria food, I guess. Sorry about that."

Miles's body had been buzzing with pure nerves since he saw her. But he was ignoring it, or at least he was trying to. He didn't sneak out of his job for a performance of *Almost Puke on Alicia*, the sequel. He could feel the rumble in his stomach, and pushed it back to the point that his hands were shaking.

Alicia noticed the paper rattling in Miles's grip. "Oh my goodness, did you come to read?"

"No . . . this . . . this . . ."

"Miles, you have to. Come on. I know you've got

something going on in there," she said looking him square in the eyes, her lisp like the saxophone playing in the store, except played by a much cooler musician. "I can see it."

Miles didn't feel himself nod, and he didn't hear himself murmur *okay*. But he did. As Dawn Leary finished her piece, the hand claps immediately sucked the fog from Miles's head and he heard Alicia tell him that she was calling him up next.

"Wait . . . what? No," Miles called, but she was already burrowing back through the crowd.

Miles took a step back. Then another.

"Thank you, Dawn." Alicia and Dawn hugged. "Y'all give it up for my girl!" Alicia commanded.

And another step back.

"Next up, we've got a newcomer. A virgin to the mic."

Another step. And another.

"So I want y'all to be kind to him. It ain't easy getting up here, sharing your soul."

One more.

"Put your hands together for Miles Morales."

Camouflage mode. Vanished into thin air.

"Miles?" Alicia craned her neck looking for him. And he was there, looking right back at her, retreating.

## CHAPTER SIX

The journey back across campus was a long and lonely one. Miles talked to himself the whole way.

"All you had to do was say no," he said.

"There's nothing wrong with just saying you're a little shy," he said.

"Or you just could've explained that you had written the poem for her," he said.

As he passed, some of his fellow students—latecomers on their way to the open mic—snapped their necks to the side, chasing the voice of a person they couldn't see. Miles hadn't taken into account that he was still invisible.

Once Miles got back to the store, before he even opened the door, he looked around to make sure no one was there to witness the door open "on its own." Once the coast was clear, Miles slipped back inside, back behind the register, back against the wall, where he climbed up, plugged the security camera back in, then reappeared just as he had planned.

His shift was almost up, and he spent the rest of it running an imaginary conversation, line for line, out loud, between him and Alicia.

*No, I can't read this in front of everyone, because I wrote it for you.*

*For me? Miles, you wrote this for me? Wow.*

*Yeah, I'm not Langston Hughes or nobody like that, but I hope you like it.*

*Oh, Miles. I love it. It's beautiful.*

And once he caught himself, he waggled his head, shook his imaginary love story out, grabbed his backpack, and closed up shop.

When he got back in the dorm, it was still empty—Miles figured by now Ganke had probably read a poem and signed up for a self-imposed encore. Normally, Miles would use the time to unwind and take his mind off of everything by tuning out and plugging in. Video games. *Super Mario Bros.*, to be exact. But tonight, he chose torture instead. He sat on the edge of his bed, reached for his bag, and pulled out Austin's letter again, this time starting in the middle and reading to the end.

I'M FIFTEEN, AND AS I'M SURE YOU FIGURED OUT BY NOW, I'M LOCKED UP. BEEN IN HERE FOR A WHILE, AND I HAVE A WHILE TO GO. I GUESS IT'S IN MY BLOOD, AT LEAST ON MY DAD'S SIDE. I'M NOT SURE HOW WELL YOU

KNEW MY FATHER. MY GRANDMA SAYS THE BROTHERS DIDN'T REALLY GET ALONG AND THAT THEY HADN'T SPOKEN IN A LONG TIME. SO THAT PROBABLY MEANS YOU DIDN'T REALLY KNOW HIM. MAYBE, IF YOU WANT, I COULD FILL IN SOME OF THAT STUFF. TELL YOU HOW HE WAS, IF YOU WRITE BACK. I HOPE YOU DO.

SINCERELY,

AUSTIN DAVIS

PS: SORRY FOR THE PENCIL. I KNOW IT'S HARD TO READ. BUT THEY WON'T LET US USE PEN IN HERE.

Miles folded the letter once more, set it on his desk. Austin assumed Miles didn't know Aaron. That the rift between brothers kept them apart. But Miles knew him well. Too well. He knew that the only reason he was Spider-Man was because of the spider in Aaron's house, stolen from the lab. He knew Aaron knew about his secret and tried to use it against him. He knew they fought, and that because of him, Aaron was dead, and Austin didn't have a father anymore.

*You're just like me.*

Miles yanked his notebook from his bag again, flipped to a blank page, and started writing.

~~Dear~~ Austin,

Thanks for the letter. ~~I have to tell you the truth.~~ I'm a little surprised. I don't really know how else to say it. I'm just so shocked. First, I guess I should say it's nice to meet you, even though it's like this. Or, maybe a better way to say it is, it's good to know you exist. I had no idea. I don't know if your grandmother told you, but I'm an only child, and I always wished there was someone for me to hang with. I always wanted a brother. Not saying you're my brother, or anything. But just that it's cool to know there's someone else in the family in my age group. I wish I would've known, ~~but the past is the past~~ but better late than never, right? Maybe we can just start fresh. Okay, some things about me.

I'm sixteen.

I'm from Brooklyn.

I go to a bougie boarding school called Brooklyn Visions Academy. I'm on scholarship, and my folks still can't afford it. A lot of rich kids acting like rich kids.

I have a homeboy named Ganke. Korean dude. Hilarious. He's the closest thing I have to a brother.

I think that's all I got.

And I ~~did know~~ knew your father. Uncle Aaron and I were close for a long time. I used to have to sneak and go see him, because my dad wouldn't allow it. That's why I'm surprised he never mentioned you, even though I guess I shouldn't be because he probably knew that if he told me, I'd want to meet you, and if we met, and got close, eventually it would be harder to keep up the fact that we all had this secret relationship. And then I would be in trouble with my dad, and so would Uncle Aaron, and I'm not sure whether or not your grandma knows about some of the epic fights between those two. Crazy.

Anyway, I guess, if you have time, write me back. This is going to sound messed up, but I don't mean it in a messed-up way—what's it like in there?

Sincerely,
Miles

PS: ~~Your father tried to kill me.~~ Maybe someday I could come visit.

Miles set the letter to the side—it was much easier to write than poetry—and lay back on the bed waiting for Ganke to come bursting in, a barrel of braggadocio, going on and on about how whatever poem he shared at the open mic turned the quad fountain into a geyser and everybody cried and clapped as water came misting down onto them. Or something like that. Blah-blah-blah. But Miles wouldn't make it. He wouldn't be able to keep his eyes open long enough to laugh at Ganke, which would then turn into Ganke laughing at Miles once he found out that Miles punked out, once again, with Alicia. Because five minutes after Miles hit the pillow, he was asleep.

Miles woke up drenched in sweat, his heart jack-hammering and his muscles tight and strained, as if they'd become ice beneath his skin. The only thing he remembered from the nightmare was that there was a cat. A cat he had never seen before. Matted white fur, its tail split into multiple tails all coiling like snakes. But Miles couldn't remember where he was and why the weird cat was there.

Miles sat up, stretched the stiff out of his joints, rubbed his eyes until they adjusted to the sunlight. He tried to remember what or who else was there in the dream. Was it Uncle Aaron? Maybe. Probably. But he wasn't sure.

He got up, crept past Ganke, who had his covers yanked over his head, and went to the bathroom to brush his teeth and wash up. When Miles returned to the bedroom, Ganke pulled the blanket back from his face.

"What you doing up this early?" Miles asked.

"Not sleeping. Lot on my mind," Ganke replied.

"You and me both." Miles grabbed his jeans off the back of his desk chair.

"What about you? What you doing up?" Ganke asked, then went straight into a yawn.

"I have to go to the store to get a stamp and envelope so I can mail this off." Miles picked the letter up off the desk. "It's a letter to Austin."

Ganke nodded. "And you sure you wanna do that?"

"I mean, what bad could it do? If he's telling the truth,

I get to have a cousin. If he's lying, I get to be a friend to somebody locked down. And it only costs me a dollar."

"A dollar, huh?" Ganke said, sitting up clearing the sleep from his throat. "I'd argue it's cost a little more than that. You think maybe you're doing this because of what happened with Aaron?"

Miles dabbed deodorant under his arms. Then, without responding, he grabbed a black T-shirt from a drawer and pulled it over his head. He went to the mirror. White skid marks down the side of his shirt from the deodorant. Of course. *Ugh.* He licked a finger and started scrubbing the fabric clean. After that, he brushed his hair, rubbed his thumbs across the stubble growing in around his hairline. Then, he snatched the letter off the desk and picked his backpack up off the floor. "I gotta go."

Miles was never outside that early, and he was surprised at how peaceful it was. The leaves on the trees were fading from green to reddish-orange, like nature's new color scheme for army fatigue. There was a crispness in the air, a breeze causing a whir all around him. It reminded him of early mornings in his neighborhood before everyone and everything was awake. Before sirens, and bus motors, and old-school soca blared from open windows. And as Miles walked across campus to the store thinking about the disaster the day before—possibly the worst Monday of his life—he reveled in the peace.

Until he got to the store.

The door was propped open and the campus police were inside interrogating Winnie.

"Just so we're clear, you've had no customers this morning?"

"Sir, I told you. I came in a little while ago. I opened the door, did my usual inventory check to see what needed to be restocked because that's usually what I spend my time doing during my shift since nobody is shopping this early in the morning anyway." Winnie scratched her scalp through the silk scarf wrapped around her head.

*No one's shopping ever,* Miles thought, but his snark was interrupted by the officers noticing him in the doorway.

"Son, no one's allowed in the store right now. It's under investigation," an officer who looked too young to be balding barked. He held up the *Halt!* hand.

"Investigation?" Miles asked, his voice seesawing between concern and sarcasm. Miles's eyes shot from the officer to Winnie.

"Yeah, I came in and all the cans of sausage were gone. Like, all of them. So I pulled up the inventory report because I couldn't believe we sold them, and I was right, there were no sausages sold, which meant they were stolen."

"Or vanished," Miles said, now half nervous, half joking.

The officer cut his eyes at Miles. Cocked his head to the side, unamused.

"Wait." Winnie looked like she was connecting the dots to something, dots that Miles had no clue needed connecting. "Maybe y'all should talk to him," Winnie said pointing at both Miles and the officer. "Miles, weren't you working last night?"

"Yeah," Miles said, the words needling his throat. He glanced back at the young baldy, caught his steely eyes, then looked away. "But nothing happened."

"Oh, *something* happened," the officer said. Miles was perplexed, watching the young officer lick his chops. Nothing happened last night. At least, nothing in the store. But something was happening now. Something bad.

With a pen and pad at the ready, the officer started in on a string of questions, each one making Miles more and more nervous. "What time did you get to work?"

"Four."

"About how many customers would you say you had?

"None."

"Any suspicious behavior?"

"From who?"

"Did you ever leave the store for any reason?"

No answer.

"Did you ever leave the store for any reason?"

"No."

"Did anyone look suspicious outside?"

"I just told you I didn't leave the store."

"Just checking. What time did you leave?"

"I *didn't* leave."

"I mean, when was your shift over?"

"Around seven."

"Cool. If we have any more questions, we'll find you."

After the officer left, Miles tried to remember if he noticed anything different about the store when he'd returned from the open mic. The truth was, he hadn't checked. Why would he? For one, his mind was on a bunch of other things: Alicia. Austin. Furthermore, the store didn't seem different. Nothing was ever moved or rearranged. The notepads were along the wall. The pens and pencils behind the register. The sausage in the back. The only reason Winnie did the inventory report was because she had to in order to keep her job, not because it made any sense. Miles racked his brain for a moment, standing smack in front of the counter, before Winnie finally snapped him out of it.

"Miles?" she said. Then repeated, "Yo, Miles?"

"Yeah." Miles blinked out of his daydream.

"Did you need something?" Winnie was perched on her elbows the exact same way Miles was the night before. Like a yoga pose—bored-convenience-store-worker pose.

"Oh . . . yeah. Just a stamp and an envelope."

Winnie turned around, ripped a stamp off a roll, and grabbed an envelope. Slid them both across the counter.

Miles pulled a crumpled dollar from his pocket.

"Thanks," he said, turning.

"What happened here last night?" Winnie prodded. "Like, forreal. I ain't gon' say nothing if you or Ganke loves those nasty sausages." She shrugged like she knew Miles had taken them, though he didn't.

"Winnie, you a sko-low like me. You of all people know I wouldn't risk my scholarship for canned meat."

"True." She nodded. "Well, it probably won't be nothing. I mean, all those cans stolen only equals about fifteen dollars. They can just bill you or your folks for that. I just had to report it because if I didn't . . ."

"I know." Miles understood. "I know."

But he *didn't* know there would be a knock on Mr. Borem's door halfway through calculus. And that Mr. Borem would turn back to the class and call Miles's name.

"A gentleman would like to see you," Mr. Borem said, always calculated. And when Miles stood, Mr. Borem added, "You'll want to take your belongings."

From there, Miles was escorted by a different campus police officer down the hall, out of the main building, across campus, and into the admin building, where he was seated in the lounge outside the dean's office—the waiting room of discipline. Miles slumped in a chair made of dark wood and burgundy leather until his mother and father showed up.

"What's going on?" Miles's mother asked, her face a knot of confusion.

"I don't know," Miles said.

"Did you do it?" his father asked.

"Do what?" Miles furrowed his brow, narrowed his eyes.

"Steal."

"Steal? Of course not! They think I stole that stuff?"

"What do you think we're—" Before Miles's father could finish preemptively scolding Miles, Ms. Fletcher, the secretary, spoke over him.

"The dean will see you now."

Five minutes later, Miles sat in Dean Kushner's office in front of a big wooden desk carved with ornate designs similar to the ones on the good china at Miles's parents' house. Dean Kushner was a small man, and looked even smaller behind that desk. He had a perfectly round, pale bald head, the veins in it like stitches in a brand-new baseball. He wore small circle-framed glasses—of course—that were the exact size of his wide eyes. The guy was a mess of circles in a wool suit.

Miles's parents sat on either side of him, their faces twisted. Both of them twitched their legs nervously. For Miles, this was even more of a nightmare then the ones involving Uncle Aaron. At least those all ended with him waking up, snapping out of it. But this was real. He had only been back to school one full day and was already teetering on another stretch of punishment. A much, much worse punishment.

"Please read this aloud," Dean Kushner commanded, handing Miles a piece of paper.

Miles glanced at the paper, gnawing his bottom lip. He sighed, glanced up at Dean Kushner, then reluctantly cleared his throat and began.

" 'Dear Dean Kushner,

" 'My name is Miles Morales. I'm thirteen years old and from Brooklyn. I have an amazing mother and father who love me more than anything, which I know might seem strange for a teenager to admit. But I know what they've sacrificed for me and what they continue to sacrifice for me to stay on a direct path to success, and it's because of their guidance that I've maintained a four-point-oh GPA in middle school. I've been taught how to be excellent, which is why I'm interested in attending Brooklyn Visions Academy, a school that also prides itself on excellence.

"'But I also pride myself on honesty. And if I'm being honest I have to also mention that even though I have a great family, I know there are people who look at us a certain way. The reason why is because my father wasn't always the man he is today. He was a person who didn't have anyone to steer him away from the traps of our community. Even though my neighborhood is a beautiful place to grow up, sometimes it can get complicated. And my father and his brother fell victim to the street, becoming teenage thieves, bringing problems to our neighborhood, and all of New York City.

"'And even though my father, with the help of my mother, pulled himself out of that situation and cleaned his life up, his brother did not. My uncle continued to break the law, hurting people, until finally it caught up to him. This part of my family is also a part of me. The same fearlessness that led them to crime is what leads me to excellence. And my goal, if you give me the honor of attending Brooklyn Visions Academy, is to continue to prove that. I believe it's not just about where you're from, Dean Kushner, but also about where you're going.

"'Thank you for your consideration, and I look forward to your reply.

"'Sincerely,

"'Miles Morales.'"

Miles set the paper back on the desk. Defeated.

"Now, Mr. Morales," Dean Kushner said, pushing his

glasses up onto the bridge of his nose. "Is this or is this not the letter you submitted with your application to this institution?"

"It is, sir," Miles said.

"And did you or did you not say that you wouldn't fall victim to the toxic patterns of your family?"

"Excuse me, Dean Kushner, but I don't think—" Miles's father interjected.

"I'm just paraphrasing what your son wrote, Mr. Davis." The dean tapped the paper.

"I understand that, sir, but—"

"Um, *we* understand that, sir," Miles's mom stepped in to massage the moment. "But Miles said he didn't do it."

"I didn't. Why would I steal something from the store I work at? And steal what? Sausage?"

"Dean Kushner, is there any proof?" Miles's father asked, still fuming over the dean's accusations.

"Well, funny you should ask, Mr. Davis, because actually there's the footage from the surveillance."

*Footage?*

Miles's father cut his eyes at Miles. "Footage?" Miles wanted to breathe a sigh of relief because this evidence should've, in fact, cleared his name. But his muscles were still tight with confusion—there was no way he could be on film stealing sausage because *he didn't steal any sausage! Right?* So why was he still so nervous?

"That's right." Dean Kushner got up from his desk and opened a cabinet to the left of him, which housed a television. He grabbed the remote, powered-on the monitor, and cut right to the scene of the crime. "Here, Miles is in the store. Now, you'll see he backs up until he's out of camera shot for a few seconds, and then suddenly, he's back," the dean explained like a lawyer in a courtroom drawing attention to *Exhibit A.*

"Okay . . ." Miles's father said.

"Dean Kushner, this doesn't really show much," Mrs. Morales said.

"Ah. But it does." Dean Kushner almost sounded cheerful. "Take a look at the time stamp. It jumps from six thirteen to six forty-four. Now, I don't know how or why the camera cut out like that, but it would be silly to believe it was a coincidence. And quite frankly, if Miles didn't steal anything, surely he should know who did because he would've been standing right there." Dean Kushner tapped the TV screen. "It only makes sense that he somehow, during the thirty minutes the camera was down, stocked up—"

"On *sausage?*" Miles snapped. He couldn't believe what he was hearing. He looked at his mother and father, their faces sour with uncertainty.

"Miles," his father said. "Just tell me you're not trying to protect anybody. If you didn't do this, then tell Dean Kushner who did."

"I don't know who did it."

"That's because *you* did it," the dean said matter-of-factly. "Just tell us the truth, son."

Miles's father drew a breath. His mom stepped in again.

"Sir, with all due respect, can you give us a moment?"

She turned to her son, lowered her voice as if she could somehow have a private discussion without Dean Kushner hearing. "Miles."

"I didn't do it." Miles's head was swiveling back and forth between his parents. "Why would I steal that stuff?"

"Maybe to sell it in the dorm. Strip and flip just like—"

"No . . . that's not . . . I didn't . . ." Miles pleaded.

His father sighed. "Miles, son . . . please."

"Dad, I really, really don't know who did it." He looked at his mother. "Ma . . ." His mother shook her head.

"Well, then, I'm not sure what other choice we have," Dean Kushner said, pointing the remote at the TV, clicking it off. He picked up the personal statement Miles had submitted with his application, glanced at it again. "As you wrote in your own words, you could have chosen to rise to excellence," the dean said, shaking his head. Miles's father clenched his jaw. "Such potential to break the chain," he continued. Miles's father now gripped his chair and tapped his foot more intensely. "But unfortunately it doesn't look like that will be happening." Dean Kushner let the paper fall from his hand.

"Wait." Miles spoke up. His parents perked up. Dean Kushner looked up. "I left the store. I didn't steal anything, but I left for . . . a few minutes."

"What?" Miles's mother said.

"You did *what*?" from his father.

A childlike embarrassment washed over Miles. The kind he used to feel when he wet the bed when he was a kid. "I just . . . I just wanted to check out the open mic. So I cut the camera, and . . . left the store." Miles dropped his head dramatically, pressed his chin against his chest, and rocked back and forth, deflated.

Miles's parents glanced at each other.

"Are you sure you're telling us the truth, son?" Miles's father asked, his voice dipping into further suspicion.

Miles lifted his face. "Dad, I'm not lying. That's what happened," he said. His father nodded, then looked back at the dean.

"Well," Dean Kushner started. He rubbed his round jaw. "Without further proof of who actually stole the items from the store, I suppose I can't expel you, son. Not this time." Miles's mother instantly relaxed her shoulders, relieved.

"Oh, thank you, Dean Kushner," she said, her hands clasped together, followed by, "Gloria a Dios."

"But." The dean whipped the glasses from his face and pointed them at Miles. "You're fired from the store, and the work-study program. I'm sorry, folks, but, effective immediately, your room-and-board voucher has been rescinded."

The post-meeting walk was a silent one. Just the sound of hard soles and high heels clacking against the pavement. Once they all got to the car, Miles's father got in the driver's seat. "We'll talk about this later," he said in a gruff tone. Then he closed the door.

Miles's mother gave him a cold hug. "I'm sorry. I didn't mean for . . ." Miles's voice began to crack. His mother didn't respond. She just tightened her lips like she had something to say, and then released him. "I guess I'll see you this weekend," he said, low, as she climbed in on the passenger side.

Miles caught the tail end of Ms. Blaufuss's class. He handed her his pass and took his seat.

"Where were you?" Ganke whispered in Miles's ear. Miles didn't say anything. Just shook his head.

"Miles, we're sorry you missed the fabulous poems about family," Ms. Blaufuss said. "But just to catch you up, the homework assignment tonight has to do with even more family exploration. I want you to either call your parents or search online for the meaning of your name." *Great.* If there was one thing Miles didn't want to do, it was call his parents. About anything. Ms. Blaufuss fiddled with the plastic bracelets on her wrists and continued. "It can be your first name, your middle name, your last name, it doesn't matter. And if you can't find any actual meaning, then ask your folks why they named you what they did. Then write a sijo on your findings. Got it?"

Miles offered a slight nod, still reeling from what had just happened in Dean Kushner's office. He sucked his lips into his mouth and pinched them down. He felt like he wanted to cry. Or scream.

The bell rang.

"Bro, where were you?" Ganke asked. "I needed you to talk me off the freakin' ledge. Everyone was talking about how much they love their families. And, I mean, I love mine too, but . . . y'know. People were talking about their dads the same way they talk about their dogs. And all I kept thinkin' was, where the hell is Miles?"

"Kushner's office. With my folks." Miles hadn't even taken anything out of his backpack, so he just threw it over his shoulder and watched Alicia walk out of the room without even looking back at him.

"With your parents?"

"Yeah. I'll tell you about it later," Miles grumbled, now moving through the grid of desks.

"Wait, you're not coming to lunch?"

"Nah, I'm not hungry. I think I'm just gonna go sit in the library until it's time for Chamberlain's class."

Ganke didn't try to fight Miles on that one. Just gave him five and walked away.

Miles ghosted down the hall in a total head-funk, his fellow classmates zipping by him as blurs of pink and peach and the occasional brown. Like Judge, who extended his hand to Miles as he approached. Miles, by sheer muscle memory, gave Judge a five as he sounded off about the Halloween party.

"Ganke said you *finally* gon' come," Judge said, the words sort of floating around Miles's ears but not actually entering. Miles was too busy thinking about what his parents might've been talking about.

*Do you think our son is a thief?*

*He said he didn't do it.*

*But do you believe him? I mean, did you tell the truth when you were stealing?*

*Sausage in a can?*

*Where was Ganke?*

*An open mic? We didn't send him there to be a rapper.*

*How are we going to pay for his room and board?*

*How are we going to pay for his room and board?*

*How are we going to pay for his room and board?*

He pushed open the door to the library and exhaled in the silence of the space. Brooklyn Visions Academy's library was like a sanctuary. It was collegiate, full of fancy lamps and tables, ornate designs in the crown molding lining the ceiling and doors. This was the library where Shakespeare and all the rest of the dead white guys Miles had to study in school would've wanted to have their ashes scattered. Under the cherrywood floorboards, or mixed into the polish of the oak tables. At this hour, everyone was either in class or at lunch, so Miles had the place all to himself. Minus the librarian, Mrs. Tripley, or as she was known around campus, Trippin' Tripley. Mrs. Tripley was who everyone expected Ms. Blaufuss to become in thirty years. An old lady full of so much life—so happy, so curious—that it seemed weird.

"Careful, Miles," Mrs. Tripley said, as Miles walked through the doors. Mrs. Tripley knew everyone's name. Every student, every teacher.

"Careful of what?" Miles said, staring up at her. "Looks like you're the one who should be being careful."

"Ah. Famous last words," she said, twisting the bulb until the light flickered on. "I just didn't want you walk under this ladder, is all."

Miles smirked. "Mrs. Tripley, I don't mean no harm, but why would I do that?"

"I have no idea, son. But people do it. And let me tell you, it's bad luck."

"I don't need to walk under a ladder to have that."

"What's that?" she asked.

"Nothing. It's just . . . You believe in that stuff?"

"What, superstitions?" She stepped gingerly down each rung of the ladder. "I don't know. I think they're interesting, and we can't prove what we can't prove, huh?" Miles had no idea what that meant, or if it meant anything at all. Mrs. Tripley continued, "But whether you believe in them or not, you still shouldn't walk under a ladder, Miles. Because somebody like me might fall on you. And that, my dear, is bad luck." She held the blown bulb to her ear and shook the burnt filament around inside. "Trust me. Been there."

Miles opened his mouth to ask, but then decided against it.

"Now, what can I do for you?" Mrs. Tripley left the ladder in the middle of the floor and walked over to the trash can behind her desk, which was also big and wooden.

"Hide me."

"Hide you?" Mrs. Tripley slapped her hands together to clear the dust from her fingers. "Are you being sought after? Are you the creature Frankenstein is chasing? Are you the young Bill Sikes being hunted by the mob of Jacob's Island? Are you Ralph running from the spears of the other stranded kids? *Hmmmm?*"

"Um . . . I'm . . . Miles."

"I know who you are, Miles. And that was Shelley, Dickens, and Golding. You, my dear, should spend more time in the library. It's not just a hiding place, but also the place where the chases happen. Understand?"

"I . . . guess so?" Miles didn't know what to say or how to respond to Trippin' Tripley, and was regretting coming into the library at all. Ganke was probably scarfing down pizza, while Miles was trying to decode the school librarian.

"Now, on a serious note, you're not really being chased, are you?" She leaned in, in case the chaser was in the building.

"No. I'm fine." What he really wanted to say was *I don't know.*

"Okay, phew. That's good." She knocked on the desk. "Knock on wood, Miles."

"I don't—"

"Just do it."

Miles knocked. "Does anyone even know where that superstition came from?"

She grabbed a pile of books from a cart beside her desk, and started toward the stacks. Miles followed behind.

"Well, I don't know if *anyone* does, but . . . *I* do," Mrs. Tripley quipped. "See, in ancient times it was believed that good spirits lived in trees, and that when you knocked on them you were calling on them to come and protect you." Then, while slipping a book onto the shelf, she added, "I'll even do you one better. You know why people say you get seven years of bad luck if you break a mirror? Because *souls* are trapped in mirrors. And when you break a mirror you let them out!" She threw her hands in the air emphatically. "I mean, I don't really believe that, and, honestly I don't know why seven is the number of bad-luck years, but that's where it comes from. Any other questions?"

"Yeah," Miles said. "You know anything about white cats?"

"Other than they're adorable? Nope."

"Nothing?"

"You said white cats, right?" Miles nodded. "Yeah . . . I got nothing."

"What about spiders?"

"They're scary," Mrs. Tripley said bluntly, while squeezing another book into an already stuffed row.

"But I mean, do you know any superstitions about them?"

Mrs. Tripley stopped between two bookshelves, turned to Miles. "I do know one thing. It used to be said that spiders could connect the past with the future. Something about the symbolism of the web."

"You serious?"

"Of course." She resumed restocking.

"How you even know all this?"

"Oh, Miles, because I live here." She caught herself. "I mean, I don't *live* here. I mean, look, sometimes I take a nap in the geography section, pretend I'm in Thailand, and wake up in the morning, but that doesn't count as living here. So . . . don't think that. But I live in the books. I read and read, all the heavy stuff, waiting for the day when one of my students, like you, comes in to ask me about . . . spiders." She checked her watch. "Now, if I were you I'd get to class."

"What time is it?"

"The first bell rang two minutes ago."

"But I didn't hear it."

"Well, the lightbulbs aren't the only things that blow out in this old place." She winked.

Oh no. *Oh no!* Miles couldn't be late for Chamberlain's class. If there was any class he couldn't be late to, it was that one. He dashed back through the stacks and barreled through the library door. The hallway wasn't packed, which wasn't a good sign because it meant the second bell would be ringing any moment. Miles broke out in a full-on sprint down the hall, rocketing into Mr. Chamberlain's classroom, sweating and out of breath.

"Made it!" he spat. Mr. Chamberlain didn't even acknowledge him. He was scribbling his daily quote over the faint outline of the quote that he'd written for the class before. When Miles got to his seat, Mr. Chamberlain began the chant for the day.

"All we ask," he said softly, "is to be let alone." He set the chalk in the chalk tray and pressed his hands together, meditatively, as the last few stragglers, including Hope Feinstein and Alicia, entered the room. The bell rang, which apparently was also the signal for Alicia to turn on her cold shoulder. Because she did.

And, like clockwork, the buzzing in Miles's head started up.

Miles opened his mouth to speak to Alicia, but the words disintegrated like snow that melts before it hits the ground. He tried again, but was cut off by Mr. Chamberlain.

"All we ask is to be let alone," Chamberlain repeated a little louder. Miles took that as a sign to let Alicia alone. Mr. Chamberlain repeated it a third time, and then asked, "Do any of you know who said that?"

"Yeah," Brad Canby said, slouched at his desk. "Everybody in this class."

Many of the students laughed, some even being obnoxious enough to bang on the desks as they howled. But Miles didn't even crack a smile. He couldn't afford to. Literally.

For a moment his mind drifted. He thought about what Tripley said about spiders representing the connection between the past and the future, and wished he could somehow apply that to getting his job back. Taking the past firing and connecting it to a future of reemployment.

*Maybe I could just beg Dean Kushner.*

*Maybe I could ask to be put on probation and given a chance to prove myself.*

*I mean, I'm basically a straight-A student. That's gotta count for something, right?*

"No, Mr. Canby," Mr. Chamberlain said, totally ignoring the disrespect. "Actually it was Jefferson Davis."

*Maybe I could—wait, what?*

And the cloud in Miles's mind instantly vanished at the sound of his father's name.

*Jefferson Davis?*

*Buzz.*

Then Miles said it out loud. "Jefferson Davis?" Managing his nausea was starting to become normal. He knew he wouldn't die. It would just feel like death, like panic, like his brain was being held over a flame and his stomach was in the spin cycle. *Spidey-sense, ignored.*

Mr. Chamberlain opened his eyes. "Morales, have you forgotten classroom decorum? Raise your hand if you want to speak." Again, Miles stared into his eyes.

"But Brad didn't . . ." Miles closed his mouth, fuming. There was no use.

Alicia shifted in her seat as Mr. Chamberlain continued. "And, yes, Jefferson Davis. The president of the Confederacy during the American Civil War. The man who appointed Robert E. Lee general of the Army of Northern Virginia, to lead the most important Confederate army." Mr. Chamberlain closed his eyes again. "The quote is a simple one, but it means so, so much. It's simply asking that the people of the South be allowed to govern themselves. That the way things were was just fine."

"Unless you were a slave," Brad blurted out, rolling his eyes.

"Seriously," Alicia said under her breath. Chamberlain opened his eyes just for a moment and shot her a glare. But he didn't say anything. Just burned Alicia with his eyes. Then he snapped them shut again, took a deep, annoyed breath, and with his hands still pressed together, and without any finger-wagging or scolding, he replied to Brad. "Well, Mr. Canby, it's a bit more complicated than that."

While Alicia shook her head every few minutes, flustered by Mr. Chamberlain's words, Miles drifted in and out of the lecture, not only dealing with the sandalwood leaping from the back of Alicia's neck, but also the fact that his father's name was the same name as the man who was fighting to keep slavery alive. And Chamberlain kept the Jefferson Davis quotes coming—*Wherever there is an immediate connection between the master and slave, whatever there is of harshness in the system is diminished*—as he preached from the front of the class to the two or three students scribbling in their notebooks and about fifteen other students who were listening to music, playing on their phones, or, like Brad Canby, had their heads on their desks, asleep. But Miles was neither writing nor sleeping. Instead he was sitting there, letting every word dagger through his mind.

"We underestimate the bond between slave and master. So many slaves were comfortable with being enslaved. Happy even. Later this week, maybe I'll bring in some images to better illustrate my point."

"Images?" Again, Alicia sparked up. "No disrespect, Mr. Chamberlain, but don't you think that's . . . I don't know . . . taking it a bit far to illustrate your point?" Chamberlain didn't budge. Alicia looked around the room for a supportive face, but most people had already checked out. She turned and glanced back at Miles, but he was staring down at the fake wood grain of his desk, fighting to keep *Are you serious?* trapped behind his lips. Too much going on. Too much at once. The buzzing was now a burning, the heat of frustration spreading throughout his body, but Miles just tapped his fingers on the desk, trying his best to keep his composure. He continued to sit, quietly stewing, as Mr. Chamberlain dug his heels into this ridiculous lecture. Miles wondered if at this point Chamberlain's Civil War lesson was all just a bait-fail, because no one cared enough to engage except Brad, who was just playing around, and Alicia, who was simply ignored. But Chamberlain kept pushing.

"An interesting way to try to understand this is to think about dogs. Dogs don't mind being on leashes—being in cages." Mr. Chamberlain, in a rare instance, broke his statue-like stance, removed his blazer and set it on his desk in the corner of the room. Then he unbuttoned his cuffs, and flipped them so that his wrists were exposed. And that's when Miles saw it. The dark outline of a cat on his left wrist. A tattoo he had seen other times but paid no attention to because Mr. Chamberlain was weird enough to have a tattoo of a cat on his wrist. The type of guy who had pet cats with complicated historical names, which he pretended were his children. *That* guy. But this tattoo was familiar. It wasn't an actual image of a cat—it was a symbol. A cat with a bunch of tails. Like the cat Miles had dreamed about the night before.

Chamberlain took a step forward and placed his eyes

right on Miles again. "And every time the dogs see their owners—the people who put those leashes around their necks, and feed them scraps—they wag their tails, happy. Some would even say . . . grateful."

*Grateful?* Miles wasn't sure because his brain had gone static, but he could have sworn Alicia had said it out loud at the exact same time he was thinking it. *Grateful?* And if she had said it, which, judging by Chamberlain's brief pause and pinched lips, she had, Chamberlain again paid Alicia no mind. No reply. But that word, combined with the tattoo on Chamberlain's wrist and the buzzing inside of Miles, was enough of a spark to light a fuse in him. Miles's tapping fingers become a clenched fist. He raised it and slammed it down on the desk, splitting the wood and buckling the metal legs. Everyone jumped, including Alicia, who whipped around to see what had happened. Miles looked into her eyes, his chest heaving.

"I'm sorry," he said softly. Then to Mr. Chamberlain, "I'm sorry."

"You should be!" Mr. Chamberlain snapped, but he didn't seem startled by it at all. As if he was expecting it. He took another step closer. "It would be in your best interest to put a muzzle on . . . this anger of yours, Morales."

"*A muzzle?*" Miles jumped from his seat, his desk crunched up in front of him. Luckily for him, at that very moment, the bell rang. Still with a closed fist, Miles looked around at his classmates, everyone wide-awake, looking on with their mouths hanging open. They slowly grabbed their bags under the heat of his gaze, as if they could be crunched up next. Miles eased his glare, collapsed his chest, collected his things as quickly as possible, and left.

As he tore into the hallway, Miles heard Alicia calling for him over his own internal voice yelling. *Stupid, stupid, stupid!* But he kept moving, juking through the mob of students, some already whispering about what had just happened moments before in class. Information moves faster in high school hallways than it does even on the internet. So Miles had to move twice as a fast.

"Miles!" Alicia shouted out again. But Miles put his head down and charged on. "Miles! Wait!" Alicia followed Miles to the end of the corridor. "Just . . . stop for one second!" she said, finally close enough to him to touch his shoulder. Miles turned around, his face tight and flushed, his chest heaving, his hands still trembling. *It's over for me. I'm outta here.* Alicia caught her breath. "Look, I just wanted to say that what happened in class today was . . . was . . . we gotta do something."

"Do something? Do what?" Miles shot back. "You wanna have a little poetry reading about it? You think that's gonna help me?" The words came out with sharp edges. Prickly. And Miles regretted them as soon as they left his mouth.

"Help you?" Alicia's face knotted. "You think this is about you, Miles?" She shook her head and sort of laughed, but not in a *ha-ha* kind of way. "This ain't about you. This is about us. And not just you and me, but about Winnie, and Judge, and all the freshmen and sophomores who are gonna have to take this class. The seniors who already have. The kids coming into this school. And if Chamberlain's acting like this, if he's talking like this, you think he's the only one? And *you* think *you* the only student he's picked on?" Alicia crossed her arms. "Maybe a *little poetry reading* won't do much, but let me ask you something, Miles, what are *you* gonna do?"

"That's not how I meant it," Miles said. "All I'm saying is, what *can* I do? You . . . you just don't know. I just . . . smashed a desk." Miles caught himself. "I mean, I . . . I just pounded it, and it broke up like that. But the point is, they're probably about to kick me out because of it. So, at this point, it don't really matter what I do."

"Oh, okay. I see," Alicia said sarcastically. "I don't know, huh? Well, let me tell you what I *do* know. You scared." Miles opened his mouth to say something, but Alicia put her hand up, stopped him. "No, no. It's okay. I understand. I don't blame you for being scared, but because you are, you just not gonna do nothing, right? Just gonna take your defeat because that's better, right?"

"Alicia . . ." Miles started, but he had nothing. No answers. No way to explain everything.

"Well, let me know how that all goes for you, Miles," she said, turning and walking away.

*Stupid, stupid, stupid.*

## CHAPTER SEVEN

"Aight, now spill it."

Miles had finally gotten back to the dorm after his afternoon classes, his stomach morphing from a tight knot to an empty pit after talking with Alicia, the same thoughts repeating over and over in his mind: *It's over for me. I'm outta here. Stupid, stupid, stupid.* Ganke had just turned on the Nintendo as Miles dug through his closet and pulled out his mask.

"Where do I even begin," Miles started. "First, somebody robbed the store yesterday," he said, flat. "While I was trying to get extra credit from Blaufuss, someone broke into—" He caught himself in a lie. No one "broke into" the store, because it was left wide open. "Someone came into the store and stole a bunch of sausage."

"What?" Ganke immediately paused the game, glanced back at Miles, who was still digging in his closet. "Sausage?"

"Yep. Sausage. In a can." Miles flung his mask and suit on his bed. "And they think I did it."

"Who thinks you did it?"

Miles rubbed his face. "Dean Kushner. My folks. That's why they came up here. They think I had something to do with it." Miles shook his head. "I mean, not for nothing, I don't even like sausage in a can."

"Who does? It's gross." Ganke unpaused the game, his thumbs working the controller as Mario jumped on bricks and onto the heads of goombas.

"Gross, stupid, whatever. It doesn't matter. Dean Kushner fired me from the store, and the whole work-study program, so now my folks have to pay out of pocket to cover my food and my luxurious life in this funk-box with you."

Ganke paused the game again, turned back toward Miles. "My man, I know you mad right now, and you just talking, but this ain't no funk-box, and if it is, it ain't because of me. First of all, you the one who wears the same jeans every day."

"That's how you break them in."

"Whatever. And second of all, I'm Korean. We don't have BO."

"What?"

"Just trust me on that one."

Miles looked at Ganke like he had two heads. "Look, the point I'm trying to make is, I can't let my parents pay for this—for my mistake. Things are already tight, and the amount of money they're probably gonna have to shell out to keep me in this dorm is gonna jam them up." Miles knocked on his forehead. "So I gotta figure something out."

"Just beg Kushy Kushy for your job back."

"Thought about that, but let's be real. When was the last time you've seen Kushner smile? I mean, he won't even loosen up his face, so why would he loosen up on me? Not to mention, none of this is probably gonna matter anyway, because I just flipped out on Chamberlain and smashed a desk. So they'll probably expel me for destruction of school property."

"You did *what*? A desk? Dude, what's wrong with you?"

"Ganke, I'm telling you, he's . . . there's something about him. I just couldn't help it. But surprisingly he didn't say nothing to me after class, or even try to stop me from leaving, so, we'll see."

"I mean, he ain't write you up, but you still might be screwed. So what you gonna do?" First from Alicia, now from Ganke. This was a question Miles was getting tired of hearing. Ganke leaned back in his chair, rested his arms on his belly. He noticed the suit on the bed. "Wait, is the sabbatical over already? Are you about to become a hero-for-hire? I hope so. Or are you just about to go find a replacement desk for Chamberlain? Which, I have to tell you, doesn't really seem like a job for Spider-Man."

"No. No. And . . . no." Miles grabbed the mask and got up from the bed. There was a mirror between his and Ganke's beds, the same mirror Miles checked out his jeans and sneakers in every day. The same mirror

Ganke used to imitate Miles checking out his jeans and sneakers every day. Looking at his reflection, he flipped the mask inside out. Pulled it down over his head, over his face. All black.

*You're just like me.*

Miles swallowed, staring at himself, but not himself.

*You're just like me.*

"I don't know." Miles yanked the mask off, flipped it back to its original side, and put it back on. He grabbed his suit from the bed. "I just need to clear my head."

By clearing his head, Miles meant going for a *jump-and-swing*, a *shoot-and-soar*. He opened the window in his dorm, camouflaged for the initial exit, and crawled out onto the wall, the black and red of his suit now the colors of red brick and mortar. Once he got to the roof, he came out of camo mode and looked out over the campus. The regal buildings and tree-lined pathways. The quad and courtyards, all emulating the Ivy League. And in the distance, the city, pushing into the sky like fingers ready to grab someone—everyone.

Miles took a few steps back, took a deep breath, sucking in everything around him, pushing all the things already in him—Dean Kushner, his parents, Mr. Chamberlain—further down. Then, he took off, and with a running start, jumped off the building.

And from rooftop to rooftop, Miles leaped as easily as if he were jumping puddles on the sidewalk, until he reached the edge of campus. Then he dove into the air, web shooting from both hands and attaching to trees, telephone poles, and any other structure around him, swinging him further into the air, high above the people below, who were scattered through the streets like ants. He didn't pay attention to where he was going, just tried to remember what it felt like to fly. What it felt like to fall knowing he wouldn't actually hit the ground.

From the clock tower to the courthouse, from the roofs of luxury condos to those of project buildings. And before he knew it, almost as if he'd suddenly opened his eyes, he was in his own neighborhood. A mash-up of sound hit him, much different than the sounds of Brooklyn Visions Academy. The screeching of bus brakes. The droning horns of taxicabs. Men hollering over bouncing basketballs. Music coming from both the radio and the sounds of the city itself.

Miles perched on the roof of the dollar store on Fulton Street—the one where Frenchie worked—and watched it all, before zeroing in on a group of kids getting off a bus, a blur of bright colors and fly haircuts that made them look older than they were. Miles watched as they walked down the block, laughing and joking, until they hit the corner. Once they reached the end of the street, they all stopped talking, passing by a group of older guys, one of whom said something to the youngins.

*Buzz. Buzz.*

Miles's spidey-sense sent vibrations around his head. *Buzz.*

The young boys didn't wait or engage. They just split,

each of them tearing off into different directions. Only one of the men broke from the crew to chase the young boys, and the one he targeted was the flyest of them all. The one with the blond patch in his hair.

Miles jumped to the next building, and the next, following along with the chase. The boy dashed down the sidewalk, sometimes jumping into the street to avoid the crowd, zigzagging from block to block while the guy followed close behind him.

And then the boy with the blond patch turned a hard left off the boulevard and bolted down a quiet street. Maybe the street he lived on, Miles thought, still lurking from on high. And with nothing in the way, the man opened his stride and ran the young boy down, grabbed him by his shoulders, and then, to play it off, put an arm around him, yoking him up. The boy didn't scream. Didn't yell for help. Miles knew that silence. The silence that knows that yelling is futile and against code. Yelling makes things more dangerous.

They took a few more steps, pretending everything was normal, until Miles noticed the young boy squatting, unlacing his sneakers.

*Buzz.*

*Read in the paper earlier that kids are being beaten up and robbed for their sneakers.* Miles's father's voice swam around his head as he jumped from the building. By the time the boy handed the thief the shoes, Miles was standing right behind him.

The boy's eyes widened. The thief turned around and met the red-and-white eyes of the spider mask. He didn't say anything. Just snarled and shook his head.

"You should mind your business," the thief said, pulling his shirt up to flash the grip of a gun tucked in his waistband.

"This *is* my business," Miles answered. He and the man faced off on the sidewalk. The young boy silently stepped to the side, climbed the stoop of one of the houses.

The man dropped the shoes. Suddenly, the tremor of Miles's spidey-sense spiked, letting him know the man was going to go for the weapon. Before he could even touch the metal grip of the pistol, Miles grabbed the man's wrist tight. Using just two fingers, he crushed the marble-like bones that help the wrist pivot, causing the thief to howl and use his other hand to brace himself. And once he had bent over in pain, Miles was right there with an uppercut, mean and clean, rocking the thief backward on his heels and onto his back. "Yeah, you act tough, but you ain't nothing but a coward," Miles said, shaking his head just before jumping on top of the guy. He grabbed the thief by his shirt collar and raised his fist. Just before Miles dropped it down on the guy's face like a hammer, he caught the kid out of the corner of his eye. The blond patch. He looked on, terrified. His eyes froze Miles, mid-bash.

*You're just like me.*

Miles stopped. He climbed off the thief, who was now just a slug, salted and shriveled up on the sidewalk. Miles grabbed the gun from the guy's pants and crushed it under his feet. Then he rolled the guy over, yanked his hands behind his back, the broken wrist now grapefruit-size. The thief yowled, and Miles held his arms together and webbed them tight.

Then he reached down and snatched the guy's shoes off. He handed them to the kid, who was shaking with fear, along with the shoes that belonged to him. "Do what you want with them." Then he leaned down and got really close to the broken and bloody stick-up man's face. "Tell everybody what just happened to you. And if you—or any of you—try it again, I will know. See, you don't know me, but I know you. And I *will* come for you."

As the kid bent down and tied the laces of his sneakers, Miles shot web up to a streetlight and swung off. He blasted web left and right, up and over, letting it randomly attach itself to various structures—light poles, high-rise buildings, construction scaffolding. While whipping through the air his adrenaline eased, and he was forced to deal with the fact that he'd just almost beaten a man to death. *What if you killed him? Right there, in front of that kid. What if you'd killed him?* Tears welled up on the sills of his eyes, but didn't fall. *What came over you? Who are you?*

*You're just like me.*

"I'm not!" Miles said, aloud, his voice muffled by the mask. Not that anyone would've heard him anyway because he was gliding through the sky on Teflon Tencel above Brooklyn. "I'm not!" he repeated, cutting the web and landing on the rooftop of a school, the momentum forcing him into a forward roll. Once to his feet, he snatched his mask from his face, his chest heaving, then peeked over the ledge as boys hung around outside the front door of the school, tall, sweaty, passing a basketball back and forth like a live grenade. They all wore practice jerseys of the school's team. A school not far from Miles's house. He hadn't been paying much attention while gliding around, but it seemed like his mind autopiloted him home. Or at least close to home. So he took the hint and decided to continue on to his house.

Miles was shocked he even thought about heading that way, because home didn't seem like a place Miles would want to go. Not after everything that had happened earlier in the day, especially since he didn't know if the news of the broken desk would be waiting for him there. But he had so much on his mind, so much he needed to figure out, that he'd rather be in the company of his upset parents in the comfort of his own home than in his stinky dorm room bombarded with the annoying chimes and dings of *Super Mario Bros.*

So, with the day beginning to dim, Miles slunk down the back wall of the school and decided to walk the rest of the way to his house in camouflage. Dogs being taken for walks would get excited when they passed him, their owners scolding them, unaware of Miles standing right in front of them making faces. A white cat scoped him out, backpedaling into attack mode, arching itself into an *n*, and hissing before dashing off under a car. But this car wasn't just any car. Actually, it was more of a house than a car. Bodega coffee cups lined the dashboard, along with random pieces of paper and trash. Garbage bags were stacked on the front seats. The sky-blue paint of the car was splotched with rust. This car was as much a part of the neighborhood as anything else. And though Miles never knew the guy's name, everyone knew that there was a man who slept in the backseat. No one bothered him. Kids spent minutes each day trying to work up the nerve to peek in at him. Today, Miles, nosy and invisible, decided to take his shot. Finally put his curiosity to rest. He peered in the back window. A tousled, striped blanket lay there alone, like a sleeping ghost. The door wasn't totally closed, and the overhead light was on. But the man wasn't there. So Miles bumped the door closed and continued on.

His block was quiet. No cars. No people. Not even Fat Tony and his boys, which was weird because they were always outside, unless cops were around. But as Miles moved farther up the street, he realized that was exactly what was going on. Police officers escorted Neek from his house. Neek, bushy-bearded and balding, looked confused, like he didn't know why he was being arrested. His face was a fireball, his mouth spouting flames.

"Let me go! Let me go!" he yelled hoarsely. "Don't let them capture me!" For a moment Miles forgot no one could see him and thought Neek was talking to him. But he wasn't. He was just yelling out. Breaking the code that had been upheld by the young man whose shoes were almost stolen. Miles figured Neek was probably having a flashback, a symptom of his PTSD. A white cat—most likely the same white cat from before—brushed its body against Neek's bottom step as the cops stuffed Neek in the backseat of the squad car and drove off.

Once they were gone, Miles climbed up the wall, over the roof, and down the backside of the house to his bedroom window. He always left it unlocked for these moments. He raised the rickety pane and slipped into his room with the grace of a ballerina. Miles could hear his parents talking in the living room and listened to them gripe, but was at least comforted by the fact that there was no *new* bad news.

Stealthily he dug through his dresser for clothes, slipping on a pair of jeans and a T-shirt over his spider suit, along with a BVA hoodie from freshman year. Each garment changed colors as he got dressed, everything blending into the wood of both his dresser and his floor. Then he climbed back out the window, back across the rooftop and down the face of the house, looking in all directions before letting the blue come back into his jeans, and the brown return to his skin.

He hit the buzzer.

"Who is it?" Miles's father's voice came crackling through the speaker.

"Um . . . it's me." Miles leaned into the talk-box.

Nothing for a second.

"Miles?"

"Yeah."

The door clicked, and Miles pushed it open and headed upstairs. His mother opened the apartment door at the exact moment he got to it.

"Miles?"

"Hi, Ma. Sorry, I forgot my key," he said, closing the door behind him. His father was just sitting back on the living room couch, bills spread out across the coffee table as if his parents were spending a cozy night alone doing a jigsaw puzzle. And in a sense, they were—trying to figure out which pieces go where. A puzzled portrait of bills.

"Almost didn't let you in. What you doing here?" Miles's father asked, cold. Miles immediately braced himself for *We just got a call from the school. You smashed a desk?*

But instead he got "You supposed to be in school, son" from his mother. Miles never thought that would sound so sweet.

"Not only are you supposed to be there, I, for one, don't want you to be *nowhere* else. I want you to be at school so much that you feel like a damn textbook."

"Jeff." Miles's mother sat on the arm of the couch, looking at him quizzically, yet still motherly.

"I just . . ." Miles started, but the words caught in his throat like a fishhook. He glanced over at the coffee table. The papers. So many of them. Numbers printed in black ink. DUE. PAST DUE. FINAL NOTICE. White envelopes stacked up at the far corner of the table. URGENT. A pencil and pad and calculator, blurring as Miles tried to speak. "I just came to say . . . sorry. I'm so sorry," Miles said, his voice cracking, his eyes now back on his mother.

"I know," she said with a sigh. "And now you've said it. We know you're sorry. But what we don't know is what's going on with you." Her eyes glassed as she stared at Miles.

*My uncle's death.*

*My school.*

*My teacher.*

*My newfound incarcerated cousin.*

*My superpowers.*

"Nothing," Miles said. "Well, I mean, I guess I just feel so much pressure. But I'm . . . fine."

"You sure?" his mother leaned in, her eyes lasering through the layers of him. Through the mask.

Miles looked away, back to the coffee table. Back to his father, who was also looking on. "Yeah." Miles nodded. "I'm sure." He gave his mother a hug. "I'll figure out how to make this okay."

"No." She pulled away. "You figure out school. Your grades. That's it. Your father and I will figure all this out."

"You shouldn't have to," Miles said.

"Oh, Miles. This is what you sign up for when you become a parent."

"I didn't!" Miles's father growled.

"Don't listen to him. Yes, we did. Papi, the two of us will starve if it means keeping your belly full. Understand?" A marble formed in Miles's throat. "Speaking of full bellies, let me pack you a sandwich to take back with you."

"And it's getting late so I'm gonna walk you to the train," Miles's father said, leaning forward. "I told you they're robbing people for sneakers. And even though yours ain't all that expensive"—he glanced at Miles's shoes—"they clean."

Outside was still pretty quiet, besides the sound of Fat Tony and his boys. They had returned to the block, and were leaning against the gate, their laughter cutting the still air.

"What's good, Mr. Davis? Miley Miles?" Fat Tony said, tossing a hand up.

"What's happening, Tony?" Miles's father said, closing the gate at the bottom of the stoop. Before Miles could speak, his father grabbed him by the arm and walked the opposite way.

"Yo, Mr. Davis?" Tony called. Miles's father turned around. "You saw what happened to Neek?"

"Yeah, I saw it."

"What you think he did?" Tony asked. Miles glanced across the street at Neek's house. The cat was now sitting on the top step of the stoop. It licked itself before snapping its head up to catch Miles's eye.

It was as if it knew Miles was watching.

It was as if it knew Miles.

"I have no idea," Miles's father said, shaking his head, and turning back around. Miles was locked on the cat. The eyes, strangely familiar. Almost magnetic. It cocked its head, studying Miles before standing up and bending into a ferocious arch of fur again.

*You're just like me,* Miles swore the cat said. Swore he saw the cat actually fix his mouth to make those words. Miles narrowed his eyes, only to see the cat was just hissing. Its tail waved back and forth, but not like normal. Most cats' tails move like charmed serpents. This one's moved like a snake's rattle. Miles's father grabbed him by the arm again, but Miles couldn't turn away. His eyes started to dry out, his vision blurring, the single tail of this feral cat splitting into several coiled tails.

The cat from his dream.

And the wrist of Mr. Chamberlain.

*Mr. Chamberlain.*

"Come on," Miles's father said. Miles tripped over his feet, turning with his father while keeping his eyes on the cat. *Mr. Chamberlain.* Miles looked over his shoulder once more as he reluctantly headed on. His brain was firing thoughts. Well, really just one: *It's Mr. Chamberlain.* He wasn't sure what that actually meant, but he knew something was up with his history teacher. Something more than just him being a jerk. But there was still so much that didn't make sense. Like, what did Chamberlain have to do with Neek? And what did Miles have to do with any of it?

"So . . . you okay?" Miles's father asked, five steps into the walk, if you could call what Miles was doing walking. He had resorted to more of a bumble. Not very Spider-Man–like.

"Uh-huh. Yeah." Miles tried to shake the distraction. He stuffed his hands into the hoodie's kangaroo pouch, then, unable to resist, looked behind him once more for the cat. It was gone.

"You don't seem like it. Anything you need to talk about? Maybe about what happened today?"

Miles swallowed the marble still lodged in his throat and turned to his father. "Do you . . . um . . . believe me?" This is what mattered more than anything. It was one thing to be accused by his dean. Another to lose the trust of his folks. "Or you think I really stole that stuff from the store?"

Miles's father sighed. "I believe you, son."

"And what about her?" Miles asked.

"Who, your mother?" Miles's father stuffed his hands into his pockets. "She's just worried about you. I mean, think about it from our perspective. Our son, who we've known his whole life, who has never been in any real trouble, got suspended from school last week for basically ditching class. And then as soon as he gets back to school, loses his work-study job for stealing. Now, I don't believe you were stealing, but you said you left to go to an open mic. My son, the math-and-science guy, leaves work to go see what? Some singing? Rapping? Poetry? You've gotta understand how this looks. You seem to be going off the rails, Miles. So, understandably, she's scared that you're going to be like . . ."

"Uncle Aaron."

"Yeah. Like Uncle Aaron. Shoot, I never thought my brother would be pillow talk between me and my wife, but something tells me that's what it'll be tonight." Miles's father stopped walking, grabbed Miles's shoulder, peered into his eyes. "Look, just tell me everything is okay."

"I'm fine."

"Then explain why you left the store. Forreal."

"I told you." Miles started walking again. His father followed suit. "I went to an open mic."

"You went to an open mic." Miles's father nodded, glaring at the side of Miles's face. "For what?"

"For extra credit."

"Ah. Okay." Miles's father nodded, then let the awkward silence balloon between them until it burst. "So . . . what's her name?"

"Who?"

"Whoever got you snoopin' around open mics, son. Look, I believe you when you say you went for extra credit. But something tells me that wasn't the only reason. You do know I was a teenager once, right? Somebody got your head spinning, unless you about to be the next Langston Hughes and I don't know it." Miles shot a look at his father, who was trying to keep a smirk from becoming a smile. "So . . . what's her name?"

Miles shook his head. "Alicia." His father chuckled under his breath.

"And does she know you like her?"

"I don't know. I thought she did, but I'm not sure now. I have two classes with her, but every time I try to say something to her I feel all queasy. At first I thought it was my stupid spidey-sense, and it might be that too, but . . ."

"But you think it's also something else. *Butterflies.*" Miles's father sang it out in a silly operatic voice, and waved his hands in the air as if conducting an orchestra, knocking up against his son.

"Whatever." Miles pushed back. "Anyway, I was *also* going to the open mic to give her this thing I wrote for her."

"So you really wrote a poem for this girl?"

"Yeah."

"Wow. It really might be butterflies. And what happened when you gave it to her?"

"I didn't. Before I had the chance to, she asked me to read it in front of everyone. And I panicked."

"Well, I'm happy to report that you got that from yours truly." Miles's father pointed to himself. "Your uncle was confident around women. But not me. You ever hear the story about how I met your mother?"

"Yeah, Ma told me y'all met at a party and how you were all smooth."

"That's how she tells it, because she's sweet. But here's the truth. It was a Super Bowl party Aaron and I were throwing at our crappy little apartment over on Lafayette. Now your mother came with her cousin, who was one of our boys. But she didn't belong there. She was a Catholic girl from the Bronx who had no business with us. But as soon as she walked in, man . . . I was done. I couldn't do anything else for the rest of the night. I don't even think I remember who was playing in the championship. All I was trying to do was figure out a way to spark conversation.

But when I tell you I was nervous . . . I was *nervous*. The only thing I figured I could do was act like a good host and serve everybody drinks, chips and salsa, and all that." Miles and his dad stopped at the corner for a second to make sure no cars were coming before they crossed. "Now, first I pour her a drink. *Champagne?*" Miles's father pretended to tip a bottle. "She thanked me and gave me a little smile. Then I asked if I could get her some chips and salsa. *Hors d'oeuvres?* But at the time I said it like this: *Or derbs?* And she said yes, again, laughing, which is always a good sign. So I go back across the room and grab the whole bowl of salsa. As I'm moving through the crowd, coming right up on Rio, I kick the side of the coffee table and start fumbling the bowl." He moved his hands around as if he were juggling invisible balls. "See where this is going?"

"You didn't."

"All over her." Miles's father nodded. They cut across the park. Shortcut. A man was lying down on a bench. Another man stopped midwalk, patting his pockets, checking for something he clearly had forgotten. A crowd of teenagers joked with each other. "A whole bowl of salsa," Miles's father confirmed.

"And what did she do?"

"Miles, did you hear me? I said I spilled a *whole bowl* of *salsa* on her. She flipped out!" Miles's father burst into laughter.

"But then . . . I mean . . . how y'all end up together?"

"Ah, that's not important. What's important is I don't think we would have if I didn't spill the salsa." He put his hands on his head, braided his fingers together. "So, that poem you wrote her, that's your salsa. You gotta spill it on her, understand?"

"Like, you mean, read it to her?"

"Exactly. Spill the salsa, son." Miles's dad's smile was self-assured, as if he knew this was a fatherly moment. A gem.

They were now on the other end of the park, standing at the steps leading down into the train station. Miles dropped his shoulders. "And what about Uncle Aaron?"

"What about him?" Miles's father snapped back into seriousness, his body tightening, his eyes lowering.

"I mean, what was *his* way of getting girls?"

Miles's father took his hand and swiped across his mouth as if wiping secret words away before they were heard. "Y'know, I don't really know. But he did it, and he did it a lot." He bit down on his bottom lip, gave a single head shake. Then he reached into his back pocket and pulled out a folded up piece of paper, slapped it in his other palm. "Guess this is as good a time as any," he said all huffy, handing the paper to Miles.

Miles unfolded it, recognized the pencil. And the capital letters.

DEAR MR. DAVIS

MY NAME IS AUSTIN. I'M FIFTEEN YEARS OLD, AND WRITING TO YOU FROM THE JUVENILE WARD. I GOT YOUR INFO FROM MY GRANDMOTHER. SHE KNEW YOUR NAME,

AND I THINK SHE FOUND YOUR ADDRESS ON
THE INTERNET. I HOPE YOU DON'T MIND.
SHE'D BEEN TELLING ME ABOUT YOU AND
SAID THAT I SHOULD REACH OUT TO TRY
TO GET TO KNOW THE OTHER HALF OF MY
FAMILY. MY FATHER'S NAME WAS AARON,
AND IF THIS IS THE RIGHT ADDRESS, THEN
YOU ARE AARON'S BROTHER. THAT MAKES
YOU MY UNCLE. I'M NOT SURE IF YOU EVER
KNEW ABOUT ME, AND MY GRANDMOTHER
TOLD ME THAT YOU AND MY FATHER DIDN'T
REALLY GET ALONG. SO MAYBE YOU DIDN'T
KNOW, OR MAYBE YOU DID BUT WAS TOO
MAD TO REACH OUT. I CAN UNDERSTAND
THAT. ANYWAY, AS I'M SURE YOU KNOW, MY
FATHER IS NO LONGER AROUND AND SO I
DON'T KNOW IF THIS IS OVERSTEPPING MY
BOUNDARIES, BUT I WOULD LIKE FOR YOU TO
MAYBE COME SEE ME. SATURDAYS ARE MY
VISITATION DAYS. I DON'T GET ANY VISITORS,
AND IT WOULD BE COOL TO SEE FAMILY,
EVEN IF WE DON'T KNOW EACH OTHER.
 I HOPE YOU GET THIS LETTER.

AUSTIN DAVIS

Miles folded the letter back up and tried to hide his
skepticism. Tried to bite his tongue. "Did you know about
him?"

"Of course not. I mean, I hadn't really talked to Aaron in a long time, and whenever I did it was to tell him to stay away from you."

"So you didn't even know this kid existed?"

"Not until this past Sunday when I opened the mail." The paper Miles's mother was holding when he'd come from the bathroom. The one that snatched the color from her face.

Miles's mind was reeling, his tongue now unbitten. "Well, I did."

"You did what?"

"I knew about him." Miles said. "I mean, not until yesterday. But, he sent me a letter too."

"To BVA?"

"Yeah." Miles handed the letter back to his father. "I didn't tell you because I didn't want you to be mad about it. But . . . yeah."

"I don't like this, son." Miles's father wagged his head, stuffed the paper back into his pocket, and folded his arms across his chest.

"We have to go see him," Miles blurted, his insides rattling.

"Absolutely not," Miles's dad snapped. "I mean . . . look, I don't know. It's not that simple."

"Well, what does Ma think?" Miles knew that his mother had a soft spot for kids and hated to see them struggling. And they didn't have to be family for her to feel for them. She loved Ganke like he was her son. But if Miles's mom knew that there was even a chance Austin could be related, despite how she felt about Aaron, she would want to connect with him. She'd have to.

Miles's father blew a hard breath, one that inflated his cheeks. "You know your mother. She thinks I should go see him."

"Well, then . . . I mean, that's it. You gotta go. And I'm going with you."

"First of all, watch yourself ordering me around, kid," Miles's father said, steely. "You still on thin ice, and punishment is not off the table. Just because you feel like you can walk out of work don't mean you can walk *on* me. Not to mention you withholding the truth."

"Sorry, sorry." Miles adjusted his tone. "But . . . well . . . since we're being honest about stuff, you should also know I wrote him back."

"You did *what*?" Miles's father gripped the top of his own head as if trying to rip it off his neck.

"I had to. I mean, it was like I couldn't help it. I just . . . did it. Dropped it in the mail this morning."

Miles's father turned away from Miles, then turned back to him and stared into the sky as if searching for the answer in the half-clouded moon. "Look, I don't know if any of this is a good idea, Miles. I mean, we don't even know this kid."

"That's why we gotta go and meet him."

"We don't even know if he's telling the truth."

Miles looked at his father, gave him an unwavering side-eye.

"Okay, okay." His dad threw his hands up. "The kid's

*probably* telling the truth. I mean, he ain't got no real reason to scam us."

"Exactly. So . . . ?"

"So, please get on the train and go back to school." Miles's father was suddenly full of frustration. His cell phone chimed. He checked it, then grabbed Miles by the back of the neck and pulled him in for a rough but loving hug, almost bouncing Miles's body off his own. "That's your mother. Let me get home so I can talk to her about it again."

## CHAPTER EIGHT

When Miles got back to his room, Ganke was sitting in front of his computer. On the desk beside his laptop lay a bag of cheese puffs.

"Hey," Miles said, closing the door behind him.

"Hey," Ganke said, without looking up from the screen. He stuck his hand in the bag and grabbed a puff, threw it in his mouth, and sucked the cheese powder off his fingertips. Then he glanced over at Miles, who inched past him. "Whoa there, Spider-Man. You left in tights and a mask, and came back in dusty jeans and a hoodie. What'd you do, take up a life of crime and rob a hipster?"

"You got jokes. But you have no idea." Miles pulled the sweatshirt over his head, the black-and-red-webbed body suit underneath. "I just came from my folks' house."

"And you're still alive, so I take it there was no second

phone call from today's classroom misadventures?" Ganke hoity-toitied his voice.

"Nah. But they're in there counting their money and calculating bills. So robbing somebody to help them out don't sound half bad."

Ganke pushed his fingers back into the snack bag, pulled out what looked like an orange Styrofoam packing peanut, and tossed it in his mouth. "Miles, please," he said. "You couldn't rob nobody."

Miles plopped down on his bed. He pulled his mask from the pocket of his sweatshirt and tossed it to the side. He wanted to tell Ganke about beating up the guy he caught trying to stick the kid up for his sneakers. How he pummeled him. How the guy's blood dotted the sidewalk. How he snatched the sneakers from the guy's feet and gave them to the kid as some kind of added justice. Miles understood that kind of vengeance. It was in him.

But he couldn't tell Ganke that. Plus, if he was being honest with himself, Ganke was right, he couldn't do it.

"Because no matter what you say, *you're just like me.*" The words slow-motioned down Miles's ear like sap and he instantly flashed back to the white cat, and from the white cat he flashed to his uncle, snarling, his hands reaching for Miles's neck. Ganke continued, "Except, of course, *I* can dance. Oh, and *you* a Super Hero, remember?" He wiped orange dust on his sweatpants.

"Man, just give me some cheese puffs. And what does your dancing have to do with anything?"

"Why don't you come *steal* them?" Ganke laughed, and held out the open bag to Miles, who snatched it. "Nah, but seriously, what if you . . . I don't know, danced for money."

"*What?*" Miles screwed his face up.

"Not like that, man. I'm sayin' . . . like, showtime."

"No."

"Miles, you've seen the kinda bread those kids get and you need—"

"Ganke"—Miles put a hand up—"I'm not pop-lockin' up and down the train for quarters."

"First of all you wouldn't have to pop-lock. And secondly, with your abilities, we'd make dollars. Not quarters."

"We?"

"Well, I gotta get my management fee. A small cut. Plus, somebody gotta collect the cash." Ganke flashed an angelic smile. "At least think about it."

Miles shook his head. There was no way. Miles definitely couldn't be a jack-boy, but he also couldn't be a subway dancer—a showtime kid. Because he couldn't dance. He had all the coordination in the world when it came to jumping across rooftops or dodging punches, but to get his body to move on rhythm was a superpower he just didn't have.

"How 'bout you think about this!" Miles shot web across the room, thick floss making a spaghetti mess on Ganke's T-shirt.

"Petty, Miles." Ganke shook his head and didn't even bother trying to peel the string from his sleeve.

Miles shrugged. "What you doin' anyway?" He grabbed the cheese puff bag.

"Researching my name for Blaufuss's homework, which by the way you still have to do. I know you needed to go get some air, or whatever it is you did when you climbed out of the window, but I just hope you breathed in some poetic inspiration. Unless you plan on trying to get more extra credit."

"Yeah . . . no. Extra credit is out." But the thought of having to write a poem at this time of night, after the day he'd had, made his head feel like it was being pinched in a vise. "This is the *what's the meaning of your name thing*, right?"

"Yep. And guess what? I don't think my name means anything," Ganke said.

Miles munched on a cheese half-moon. "Have you looked it up?" he asked, the cheese puff melting in his mouth.

"Yeah, before you got here. Matter fact I looked up a bunch of names. Like, Alicia, her name means 'nobility.' Oh, and a good one was Chamberlain. Dude, that jerk's name actually *means* 'officer who manages the household.' Ha! But the best *and* worst one was Ratcliffe. Literally means 'red cliff.' Too bad Ryan won't jump off one." Ganke waved for the bag of cheese puffs, then rambled on. "Anyway, the point is, when I looked up mine, the only thing that came up was some definition from Urban Dictionary that said it means 'kill.'"

"Kill?"

"Yeah, like . . . when you kill people, apparently you ganke them."

Miles's stone face of exhaustion cracked into a smile. Then that smile became a chuckle. "Nah, man. That's *gank*. You *gank* somebody."

"Oh, *gank*? I know *gank*. The internet said *ganke*." Ganke eased up. "I was about to say, dang, my name means *murder*?" Miles and Ganke laughed. "But forreal, my name don't really mean nothing. I don't even think it's Korean, which is weird."

"Did you call your folks?" Miles asked. The laughter that had just lightened the mood of the room was gone. Ganke's face grew heavy.

"You know I'm not tryin' to call them. Plus, call and ask them what? *Hey, did y'all just make up my name?* Nah. I mean, I could call my mom, but I just don't wanna hear her be sad, man. She'd probably be like, *Your father named you*, and burst into tears. And if I call my pops, he'd probably be like, *Why, you don't think it's good enough?* Or *It's the Lee that matters, son.*" Ganke picked up one of his sneakers and kissed it, imitating his father. "What about you? You know what your name means?"

"I'm surprised you ain't already look it up."

"Well, real friends don't let friends get out of doing their own homework," Ganke said. "But whatever. Let's see. *Miles. Miles. Hmm.*" Ganke let the name ring out while he pretended to ponder.

"I mean, it probably just means distance or something like that," Miles said.

Ganke side-eyed his friend. "That's the best you could come up with? Really? If anything, it means *desk breaker.*" He swiveled in his chair back to his laptop. His fingers clicked and clacked on the keys, then his eyes shot left to right. "Hmm," Ganke hummed again. He picked the laptop up, rolled back over to Miles and set it in his lap. "Here. Read."

Miles tilted the screen back.

*Miles /ˈmaɪlz/ is a male name from the Latin,* miles, *a soldier.*

"Soldier?" Miles's eyes narrowed, scrolling up and down the screen to verify.

"Soldier."

Miles should've known something was up in Ms. Blaufuss's class when Alicia didn't want to share her name poem. As a matter of fact, Alicia didn't participate in class at all. After the class turned in their name sijos—including the soldier poem that Miles wasn't very proud of, and Ganke's piece, entitled "Korean Untitled"—Ms. Blaufuss went on a nerd-rant about this poet, U T'ak, and this sijo he wrote about a spring breeze melting snow on the hills. Ms. Blaufuss prodded the class to respond.

"What does he mean when he says he wishes it would melt the aging frost forming in his ears?" she asked. Miles expected Alicia to answer, because he knew she understood poetry in a way most people didn't. But instead, Ryan offered his interpretation.

"The way I see it, the breeze is really like a soft caress," he said. He was met by a chorus of groans. Except for Alicia, whose face was slanted down at the notebook on her desk as she scribbled ferociously through the entire class. She and Miles hadn't spoken, which was no surprise, but Alicia hadn't really spoken to anyone. Not Winnie. Not even Ms. Blaufuss, besides a short "Hey" at the beginning of class.

After lunch—Ganke tried to get Miles to imagine what a catfish would look like if it were actually half-cat, half-fish—Miles headed to history class. He came in, took his seat at the now shaky, bowlegged desk, while Mr. Chamberlain started his usual routine of writing a quote on the board: the text of the Thirteenth Amendment. Alicia walked in among a bunch of other students, sneakers squeaking, backpacks hitting the floor, chair legs scraping against linoleum. Alicia beelined for her seat, dropped her bag. She glanced at Miles quickly, but just long enough for him to see something in her eyes. Not fear. Rage. She whipped around and strode right up to the chalkboard where Chamberlain was mid-scrawl, and picked up a piece of chalk from the chalk tray.

"Alicia?" Mr. Chamberlain eyed her as she began to write just underneath his quote in all capital letters.

WE ARE PEOPLE

WE ARE NOT PINCUSHIONS

"Alicia!" Chamberlain shouted. But Alicia continued.

WE ARE NOT PUNCHING BAGS

WE ARE NOT PUPPETS

Miles couldn't believe what he was seeing. The entire

class was silent. Even Mr. Chamberlain stood frozen in shock. Finally, he grabbed an eraser and started erasing what he could, but Alicia just moved to a different spot on the board, as if playing an intense game of tag, and scribbled on.

WE ARE NOT PETS

WE ARE NOT PAWNS

WE ARE PEOPLE

WE ARE PEOPLE

WE ARE

"That's enough, Alicia!" Chamberlain dropped the eraser. "Have you lost your mind?" He reached over and grabbed her arm, yanking it away from the board.

"Don't touch me," she said, pulling away from him. Miles lifted himself off his seat instinctively, the backs of his knees sizzling, ready to pounce. Chamberlain stepped back. Miles eased up. "Don't ever, *ever* put your hands on me." Alicia scowled, and then she began to recite what she had written out loud: "We are people. We are not pincushions. We are not punching bags."

"Go down to the office, right now," Chamberlain growled, his nostrils flaring.

Alicia turned to the rest of the class, all of whom sat with their mouths open, some, like Brad Canby, surprisingly, nodding.

"We are not puppets. We are not pets. We are not pawns."

"Get out of my class, Alicia! This is out of line. I'll have you suspended! Expelled!"

Alicia looked directly at Miles. Directly *into* him, her eyes glazing over. "We are people. *People.*" She looked back at Mr. Chamberlain. Threw the piece of chalk on the floor, grabbed her backpack, and left.

So Wednesday wasn't *totally* uneventful.

Not as uneventful as Thursday.

Miles had pretty much been on his absolute best behavior. No hangouts, his secret crush had basically *been* crushed, and unfortunately, no Campus Convenience job to go to. Just school. And wondering about Alicia. He knew she had been suspended, and he couldn't help but think about what he could've done, even if it just meant reciting the words with her. But he couldn't do that. No, he *could've*. He just *didn't*.

But she was back in class on Friday, the last day of their sijo unit. She took her seat, keeping her back to Miles. He tried to speak, but couldn't find the words. Somehow he'd misplaced his *hello*s.

Ms. Blaufuss wrote on the board in loopy cursive, *If only . . .*

"This is how I want each of you to begin your poems. You will all write one, and before class is over, we will read them one after another as a single continuous poem, the perfect cap to this unit." Ms. Blaufuss, who was wearing an old-school Janet Jackson concert T-shirt, gave the class thirty minutes. When the time was up, she started at the front of the room with Shannon Offerman and worked backward. The ongoing poem snaked through the room, jumping from issues with mothers, to the desire to have longer hair, to "If only I could love you"—that one, of course, coming from Ryan. Eventually it landed on Alicia.

"If only life weren't such a strangely complicated
     pattern,
every person in the world a single fly stuck to the web,
And fear is the spider waiting for the right moment to
     feast."

Ganke slapped Miles on the back.

"She talking 'bout you," he whispered.

"No, she's not," Miles replied, even though he felt like she might've been. But she hadn't been paying him any mind, so he pretty much spent most of his class time trying to pretend she wasn't there. Every time he met her eyes, he immediately felt like he was somewhere between naked and invisible.

Winnie was supposed to be next, but she was absent, so Miles was up. *Perfect.* He cleared the cobwebs from his throat. "Um . . ." he croaked. "I think I might've done this one wrong."

"No such thing, Miles. As good as your name poem was, I'm sure it's fine. Maybe different, but not wrong," Ms. Blaufuss reassured him.

Miles gave a half nod, stared down at his paper and began.

"If only is what's circling in my mind every morning
before I breathe in beauty and breathe out bad
    decisions;
If only is the cool breeze before I spin the world
    apart."

Miles could hear Ganke's paper rustle behind him.

Ms. Blaufuss's lips spread into a warm smile. "Very
nice, Miles. Next, Ganke."

"Skip," Ganke said.

"What? Why?" Ms. Blaufuss asked. Miles turned
around. Ganke was always eager to recite.

"I'm not ready," Ganke explained, but Miles could see
that his poem was done.

"Doesn't matter. Let's hear it. I'm sure what you have is
beautiful," Ms. Blaufuss said. She had a way of seeing the
good in everything. Everyone. Tripley with less trip. And
everybody loved that about her.

"Okay.

"If only our parents knew how much we really loved
    them,
how much we really need them to smile and look at
    each other
with eyes that say they still love each other as much as
    we do.

"That's not really how I wanted to say it," Ganke
explained.

"It's good, Ganke. It's fine. Let's keep going. Next."

Miles turned around, gave Ganke a nod.

Though the rest of the week in Ms. Blaufuss's class had been poetry, Mr. Chamberlain's class, since the battle of Alicia, had been war. Same crazy talk about the "days of old Dixie," and how after the South lost the war, they were forced to end slavery.

"Neither slavery nor involuntary servitude, except as a punishment for crime whereof the party shall have been duly convicted, shall exist within the United States, or any place subject to their jurisdiction." The Thirteenth Amendment. Mr. Chamberlain had written it on the board Wednesday, but after everything that happened, he decided to reteach the lesson Thursday. He explained how the amendment came to be, the key players (or "disrupters," as he called them) but it was Friday, after all this setup, that he drove home his main point about it.

"The *beauty* of it all," Mr. Chamberlain said, "the subtle triumph in such tragedy for the Confederacy, is this." He took a piece of chalk and raked it across the board underneath the words *except as a punishment for crime.* "See, the South rose up again, by a new, much smarter form of slavery. Prison." He smiled, and his eyes were open—a break from his typical blind-gnome stance. Actually, he had been keeping his eyes open constantly since Tuesday, since Miles crushed the desk—which, by the way, had fallen apart completely. Now only the top of the desk, no legs, was sitting on the floor. Mr. Chamberlain still made

Miles work at it, even though it was more like a step stool than a desk. And not only was he forced to be at the desk, he had to abandon his seat and squat in order for him to actually use the surface. Miles had been squatting when he'd scribbled other notes about the amendment, and tidbits of Mr. Chamberlain's rant about the forefathers who wrote it, in his notebook the previous day. And he'd been squatting today—Friday—doing the same thing, when Mr. Chamberlain decided it wasn't enough.

"It would be much easier for you on your knees, Morales," Mr. Chamberlain said to Miles. When he said it, he glanced at Alicia too. She had returned to class after a one-day suspension and Chamberlain was watching her as if he was scared she'd spring from her desk and tackle him. "You may only use a chair if that chair is sitting level with an accompanying desk, and well, seeing as though yours isn't, because you decided to destroy it, I suppose I'd have to write you up if you chose that option."

"But the only reason he—"

"Oh, Alicia." Mr. Chamberlain cut her off. "We're not going to have a repeat episode, are we?" Miles noticed Alicia's foot tapping, and even though he couldn't see her face, he knew she was biting her lip. "You know, you can always join him down there if you like."

Alicia stopped talking. Just hung her head in defeat and disgust. Miles did too. He couldn't be written up again. He couldn't be suspended, or expelled. This school was his shot. His opportunity. His parents reminded him of that.

His whole neighborhood reminded him of that. So Miles, embarrassed, got down on his knees and continued scribbling his notes using the low, legless desktop.

It took everything in Miles to not lose it. To not break what was left of the desk over Chamberlain's head. To not break him open to see if he was full of white cat fur or something. Because there was definitely something. But Miles continued to swallow it, convulsing with his screaming spidey-sense, his handwriting becoming jagged streams of ink. Along with that, he had to deal with the awkward glances of his classmates, their mouths silent— no unchecked, snarky Chamberlain jokes, no nothing. Miles figured they were now all looking at him as both a charity case and some kind of loose cannon. Making up all kinds of stories about him. A sko-low trapped in his own temper, *probably dealing with family issues.*

But before Miles could explode again, he was once more saved by the bell. Alicia immediately jumped from her seat to help Miles up. And even though it was a nice gesture, Miles couldn't help but pull away from her, upset. Small. Miles looked down, studied the floor for a second before slowly taking her face in, and letting her see his. His eyes were glassy. Hers were as well. Now he could see she was, in fact, biting down hard on her bottom lip, shaking her head, trying to find what to say.

"I . . . my family," she eked out, shaking her head.

Miles nodded. He understood. "Yeah, mine too," he replied, a baseball stuck in his throat.

Alicia turned to Mr. Chamberlain, tried to cut him with her eyes, but he turned around and began erasing the board. His back a *Don't bother.*

Alicia stormed out of the room in the midst of the clamor of squeaks and screeches. Miles followed.

"Morales, can I have a word before you leave, please?" Chamberlain said, stopping Miles in his tracks. Miles stepped up to the old man, who had taken two erasers in his hands. Got right up on him, close enough to see the white hair hanging in his nostrils, and the chafed skin outlining his lips. Close enough to take him out. "You know," Chamberlain began, "as long as you stay where you belong, in the place you made for yourself, you'll survive." Then Chamberlain took the two erasers and clapped them together, and asked, "Oh, and how's the job?" And watching Miles's face crack beneath the skin, in the midst of the cloud of chalk dust, Chamberlain added, finally, "What a tangled web we weave."

After a class like that, an experience like that, Miles needed to do something with all that rage. He could go into camouflage, kick over trash cans, put holes in walls. He could do what he'd done a few days before—go looking for trouble, save someone else from it. And do it all behind the mask, letting Spider-Man do Miles's dirty work to somehow cleanse himself. Or maybe he could approach Alicia humbly and now get on board with organizing something with the Dream Defenders. Something to speak out against Chamberlain.

But before he could decide on any of these things—*Buzz*.

A text message. Miles rammed the door of the building open, the hinges challenged by the force, and was blinded by the sun. He turned his back to block it out so he could check his phone. He figured it was Ganke asking about what happened in Chamberlain's class. But it wasn't.

**2:51pm** 1 New Message from Dad
TMW MORN

And then another came through. *Buzz*.

**2:53pm** 1 New Message from Dad
AUSTIN

And those three words were enough to help Miles get a grip and dial himself down. That and what he found when he finally got back to their dorm.

Ganke. Being Ganke.

Music was blasting. Hip-hop from the eighties. Old break-beat stuff that Ganke had found online. Stuff that Miles's father talked about whenever he was trying to prove a point about what was "real hip-hop." Ganke was stepping, sliding, and gliding around the room in his socks, ticking, popping, rocking, dancing like he had just won the lottery.

When Miles came in the room, Ganke robotted his way over to him, a silly grin on his face. He held his hand out for a five. Miles slapped it, and Ganke waved his arm up to his shoulder and down his arm again as if Miles had just sent an electrical current through him. Then, he stopped the music.

"Is this what you do when I'm not around and you're not playing video games?" Miles asked.

"Maybe. I mean, sometimes. How you think I keep this physique?" Ganke wiped sweat from his forehead, flopped down on his chair, and reclined on its back legs. "Psych, nah. I heard about what happened in the reality TV show that is Chamberlain's class, and I knew you would be in a funky mood. So I figured this would at least take some of the edge off . . . by putting you in a real . . . *funky* mood." Ganke nodded slowly.

"Thanks, man." Miles threw his backpack on his bed. Took a seat. "But I'm okay. My pops told me we're going to see my cousin . . . well, Austin, tomorrow."

"Word?"

"Yeah. But it doesn't mean seeing you pretend to be Crazy Legs— Was that his name? Crazy Legs?"

"Whose name?"

"Never mind. Just sayin' I still appreciate you trying to make me feel better, dude."

"Well, to be honest, it was for me too," Ganke said. "Man, it's Friday. And you know better than anybody that that means I gotta go home to my weird house." Ganke cracked his knuckles, stared at his own reflection in the black screen of the turned-off television. "And guess what, because I'm not going to be around on Sunday, my pops is gonna come over tonight to do, like, the family dinner thing. So my Friday night will basically be the three of us sitting there quiet, eating kimchi jigae. And trust me: the pork and potatoes and all that is good stuff, but it don't taste the same when nobody's talking. And I bet it's gonna taste even worse with all this happening on a Friday. A *Friday*, Miles."

"Yeah, I hear you."

"It sucks. So I just needed to get it out, y'know."

Miles thought of all the plans that had been running through his mind before the texts from his dad. "Yeah, I do."

Ganke turned to Miles. "You should try it."

"What . . . no. Nah."

"Come on, man. It's just us in here." Ganke got up and turned the music back on, the bass thumping, bouncing off the plastered walls. He bobbed his head. "Let me see what you got, homie. Just let yourself go." Ganke shook out his arms, while Miles crossed his.

"We have to go." They had a train home to catch.

"We will. As soon as you hit me with a move."

"I know what you doing, Ganke."

"What? Trying to help my friend chill out? Trying to help a dude I consider my brother remember that life is still good? Trying to remind the great Miles Morales that nothing can stop him, and that's cause for celebration? What's wrong with that?"

"Whatever." Miles sighed because he knew Ganke

wouldn't stop until he complied. And he needed to get off campus as quickly as possible. "Let's just get this over with."

Miles stood up, rolled his neck from right to left, left to right to loosen up.

"Just feel the music, bro," Ganke said encouragingly. Miles bobbed his head to the beat, and when he felt like he'd caught it, he started to do . . . something. One leg shot out, then the other, like some kind of Irish jig. His arms, stiff as boards, swung out in front of him like a zombie's. It was bad. *Bad.* So bad that Ganke immediately cut the music, while Miles was mid . . . um . . . lurch.

"You know what? This was a bad idea. Let's just go."

Rush hour. Friday. That meant a packed train with no seats. Miles and Ganke crammed in and held the railing above their heads, smaller people nestled into their armpits, bigger people with their hands planted flat on the ceiling of the train car. Most had earbuds in, books fanned open, or were talking to someone beside them.

"So, about this Halloween party tomorrow," Ganke said. "You still goin', right?"

"Why you keep asking me that?" Ganke had been bugging Miles about it every day that week. He had already made up in his mind that Miles would back out. And Miles had thought about it, was on the verge of flaking until he realized Mr. Chamberlain would be at the party, and he was *buzz worthy.* If it meant Miles had a chance to crack the Chamberlain code, there was no way he was missing the party.

There was only one problem.

"Have you even asked your folks?" Ganke knew Miles well.

"I keep forgetting, but I will."

"Do you even know if you're allowed out of the house this weekend? I mean, you lost your job. And then the next day you broke a desk with your bare hands."

Miles glared at Ganke, who shot back a *just sayin'* face. The commuters all swayed with the rocking train. Everyone but Miles.

"You don't have to keep reminding me. Anyway, I'm going, Ganke."

"Okay, good. Then I should tell you that I've decided that in your honor, I'm going as Spider-Man," Ganke said low, keeping a straight face. "Just let me hold your suit. It's spandex, right? It'll stretch." Ganke paused. "Unless, of course, you were planning on going as him. You."

"Whatever." They both laughed. A blind man snaked through the crowd, his cane tapping against the shins of many of the riders. He shook a jangling cup, and begged, "Can you please spare some change? Can you please spare some change?"

"What you think?" Ganke whispered as the blind man approached. Miles concentrated on the old man, studying the hesitation in his movements, the muscles around his eyes. Miles nodded at Ganke. They both put dollars in his cup.

As the train pulled into Prospect Park, people poured through the doors, allowing space for Miles and Ganke to breathe. Elders and teenaged jerks snatched up seats, sometimes squeezing in the sliver between an earbudder and reader. Miles and Ganke moved their hands from the railing to the pole as the doors closed. And then . . .

"Good afternoon, ladies and gentlemen. We hate to disturb you on your way home and actually have come to provide the perfect start to your weekend. Most of you know what time it is, but just in case you in from out, or up from down, we welcome you to our crazy town with . . . SHOWTIME!" A young boy with a raspy voice came strutting up the aisle bare-chested, his T-shirt wrapped around his head, his hands cupped around his mouth.

"SHOWTIME!" two or three other boys shouted in unison.

"Showtime!" Ganke yipped, bouncing his eyebrows at Miles.

The music started, and then came the clapping. "Pay attention!" the young one shouted, as one of the older dancers started with the footwork. From there came flipping, handstands, pole tricks, and tourists looking on in awe, their mouths hanging down to their laps. Fingers in pockets and purses.

Thirty seconds later, the showtime boys yelled, "That's our show!" The shirtless boy started clapping again, the train joining in. He ran up and down the aisle with a hat to collect the donations from the onlookers. Ganke held a twenty-dollar bill in the air, but when the kid got to the end of the train where he and Miles were standing, Ganke wrapped his fingers around the money.

"Let's have a dance-off for it."

"Ganke, don't," Miles whined. "Kid, he doesn't—"

The kid looked up at Ganke. It was like he didn't even hear Miles. "And why would I do that? I already got this money." He shook the hat lightly.

"Because you just got about ten dollars from this car. I have double that in my hand. Either you walk away with thirty, or you walk away with ten. You can't lose. It's a safe bet."

"And it's me against you?" the kid asked. "What I look like, a fool?"

Ganke chuckled. "Okay, the best one of y'all."

The young boy called the rest of the crew out. Miles tried to shut it all down, but Ganke kept waving the twenty around, which pretty much made Miles invisible.

"Aight, let's do it. Me against you," the captain of the showtime crew said. He was a wiry kid with braids and big earrings that were obviously fake diamonds.

"No, no, no. You guys got to choose *your* best, so I get to choose *mine*." Ganke threw an arm around Miles. "Him."

"He's just playing. He's gonna do it himself. I'm not a d-dancer," Miles stammered.

"Yeah, you don't really look like one," the young boy jabbed. "You either," he said to Ganke.

Ganke instantly went into a body roll. "Don't try me," he warned. "But he's better." Ganke leaned over to Miles and whispered, "Just don't do what you did in the room." Then he turned toward the showtime guys and said, "Hit the music!"

The beat came blaring from the janky handheld stereo again. A loop of some kind of electronic song Miles had never heard. Then came the clapping.

"Take two, ladies and gentlemen. A friendly competition!" The kid with the braids began contorting his body, almost knotting himself on beat. His limbs, long and noodly, were surprisingly strong as he jumped up, grabbed the ceiling rail, and air-biked down the train car.

"Give me your bag," Ganke said, practically snatching it off Miles's back.

"Your turn," the young boy said.

"Dude, what in the world have you gotten me into?" Miles asked, but before he could say anything else, Ganke pushed him into the invisible dance circle. Everyone watched. Even the New Yorkers, who were accustomed to ignoring this kind of thing. Older black men glanced over their glasses, smirking. Young white ladies sat with their hands in their laps in anticipation. Little kids clapped off beat.

"Go! Go! Go!" Ganke said. Miles froze. And then, against Ganke's suggestion, Miles broke into his weird convulsion dance, his legs and arms going every which way, his face contorting far more than his body, which seemed to have become stone. The kids burst into laughter.

"Uh, he's just warming up," Ganke said. He turned to Miles. "Do the wall crawl."

"The what?"

"The *wall . . . crawl.*" Wink-wink.

And that's when Miles got what Ganke had been saying

this whole time. He turned his back on everyone and broke out running down to the end of the train, weaving between the poles. Once he got there, he jumped and kicked off the door—the one leading to the next train—and crawled on the ceiling of the train down to the other end. No railings. Just fingers and feet.

Everyone in the car went wild, erupting in a mixture of excitement and confusion. Even the young dancers were clapping and nodding. They cut the music, waving their arms and shouting, "It's over! It's over!"

Ganke put the twenty back in his pocket, then opened his backpack and trotted up and down the train car, collecting money from . . . *everyone*. Even the showtime boys gave him a dollar.

The young dancers glared quizzically at Miles. They even attempted the wall crawl, ridiculously trying to grip the ceiling before realizing they were wasting their time. Eventually the kids left the train and went to the next car for the next show as Ganke yanked bills from his bag and handed them to Miles.

"How much is it?" Ganke asked.

"Around forty bucks," Miles replied in disbelief.

"Ahem," Ganke said as the train pulled into the Atlantic Avenue stop, where Miles needed to get off to catch the C train to Lafayette. Miles peeled four bucks from the wad and slapped it in Ganke's hand. "My fee is twenty percent. Also, this is gonna be the only fun I have tonight before the *dinner of doom*, so . . . c'mon." Miles slapped another four in Ganke's palm, stood up and threw his bag over his shoulder. And as Miles dashed for the door, pushing out as people were pushing in, Ganke shouted at Miles's back, "Told you so!"

Thirty dollars richer, Miles walked through the park toward his house. In the late afternoon, the old men played chess and blasted soul jams from a parked car's window. The little kids wobbling on their bicycles with uneven training wheels. First loves kissed on the wooden benches—soon to be beds for the homeless—next to the old ladies giving out church pamphlets. A breeze was in the air, and the trees in the park swayed, their leaves whispering to Brooklyn.

Miles passed the dog walkers, walking both pit bulls and poodles. People coming in and out of the corner bodega, the door chiming over and over again. Fashion folks draped in the latest trend snapping pictures in front of a sky-blue, rusted-over car. The one that used to be a home for someone. A man that was no longer there.

He went on past his house, down the block, and around the corner to the market. Not the bodega, but the actual grocery store. Flowers in buckets lined the front. One of the men who worked at the store was tending to them.

"How much?" Miles asked, checking out the roses.

"Fifteen," the man spat.

Miles didn't say anything else. He just kept walking. Roses would've been nice for his mother. But that would've been half his money. He knew he could've gone in the store and bought actual groceries, which would've been smart, maybe even convince his father to cook dinner for his mom for a change. She deserved it. But disasters come in all forms, and Miles and his father attempting to make a meal would've been nothing less than a disaster. And even if it weren't, it would've resulted in Miles's mother standing over them, her hand to her forehead as she gave orders in Spanglish and repeated over and over, "Alluda me santos." Help me, saints.

Miles had other plans.

The next stop was the dollar store. An older lady held the door open for him as Miles slipped into the land of paper plates, party favors, greeting cards, and the off-brand version of pretty much everything else ever invented. Shaky-wheel carts rattled, registers *blooped* with each scan, plastic bags *shished*. Miles bopped around, peeking down each aisle, before spotting Frenchie. She was squatting down, putting price tags on bathroom air fresheners.

"Hey, Frenchie."

"Miles?" Frenchie looked surprised to see him, which made sense since Miles was rarely around. "What you doing in here?"

"Lookin' for flowers."

"Flowers?" Frenchie stood up with a smirk, crossed her arms. "I know you ain't old enough to be dating yet. I remember when your daddy used to pay me to babysit you, and you ain't do nothing but pee on yourself, non-stop. Now you in here looking for flowers."

"Not for no girl. I mean, not for . . . It's for my mom."

"Uh-huh. Better be," Frenchie teased. "That's sweet. I hope Martell is as thoughtful as you when he gets older."

"Oh, he's gonna buy you a whole rose garden when he gets to the league."

"Heyyyy, you ain't said nothing but the truth!" Frenchie put her hands in the air and closed her eyes, like she was sending up a three-second prayer. "Come on."

She took Miles to the other end of the store, where the flowers were.

"Right here." She pointed at the row of greens and browns and reds and yellows, all of autumn in aisle two.

"Y'all don't have real ones? These plastic," Miles said pinching the fabric petal of one of the fake roses.

"Kid, you at the dollar store," Frenchie shot back. Miles picked up one of the roses, smelled it, and immediately felt stupid for doing so. Frenchie added, "But just so you know, these *two* dollars."

After Miles bought the rose, he went next door to Raymond's Pizza, not to be confused with Ray's Pizza. They weren't the same. Miles figured it would be safer for Raymond to make dinner for the Morales family than for Miles and his father to. Pizza always works and doesn't require saints.

People lined the counter placing orders by the slice.

"Two regulars."

"Let me get a pepperoni."

"A regular and two sausages, please."

The men behind the counter cut the pizza into slices, slid them into a big oven to be heated for a few minutes before sliding them back out onto paper plates and pushing the plates down the counter to be bagged up.

"Next!" the guy behind the register called out while slamming the cash register drawer.

"Let me get a whole pie. Regular," Miles ordered.

"Whole pie, got it," the man repeated. Then he moved on to the next person, a dude who looked a little older than Miles.

"Y'all got anchovy?" the guy asked.

"All outta anchovy, pa-pa." The thought of anchovies on pizza immediately made Miles think of his uncle, and ordering pizza at the Ray's by the Baruch Houses. A shudder shot through Miles's body.

"Aight, well, let me just get a pepperoni. Well-done."

About five minutes later Miles's pizza was being shoveled out of the oven and into a box. It came sliding down the counter.

"Regular pie, right?" the man behind the register asked.

"Yep."

"Fifteen." Miles put his money on the counter, grabbed his box, and headed for the door, walking behind the guy who asked for the anchovy slice. But the door was being held by someone else. Someone familiar. At first Miles couldn't place him, but as they all started walking, the anchovy dude first, the door holder stalking behind him, and Miles bringing up the rear, Miles realized who the middle man was. The thief, his face still black-and-blue from the lesson Miles taught him. Miles noticed the guy, who was now holding his pizza slice up to his mouth, was wearing brand-new sneakers. Air Max infrareds. The same ones Ganke had on at the basketball court. Miles's spidey-sense buzzed. The thief kept looking to his left, and to his right, making sure no cops were around. Or no Spider-Man.

The jack-boy turned around.

But it was just Miles, as Miles, glaring back at him. And when they got to the corner, the thief cut off to the left. The guy with the pizza and sneakers kept straight. And Miles went right.

Miles climbed the stairs to his house, pizza and rose in hand. He could hear music coming from the other side of the door. He jiggled the key just right to unlock it, and was met by his mother and father in the living room, dancing hand in hand. Horns, cowbell, timbales, and conga drums blaring through the speakers. Salsa. The Fania All-Stars.

"Hey, Miles," his mother sang out, back-stepping, whirling her arms around. His father reached out for her, and she took his hand just for a moment, before letting go and whipping into a spin. Celia Cruz's voice wrapped around them like a warm quilt as Miles's father pulled his mother close for an awkward dip.

"Rio, the boy has come bearing gifts," Miles's father said, pulling away from his mom.

"Um . . . I got a pizza." Miles was in shock. He set the box on the kitchen table. He wasn't expecting his folks to be dancing and laughing. Not that they never did, Miles just figured after the week they had all had, he'd find them in the house staring at the TV, still discussing bills, waiting for him to get home to figure out a possible punishment.

"Pizza!" Miles's mother squealed. "So sweet, mijo. Thank you."

"Did you steal it?" Miles's father asked, lifting the lid, the cheesy steam wafting up to his face.

"Does it matter?" Miles joked lightly, as his father stuck his finger in a glob of cheese.

"Nope."

*So far so good.*

"And I got this for you." Miles held the rose out toward his mother.

"Me?" She played coy. "I thought that was for your girl at school. Tu amor."

"No. It's not. Plus, I don't have a girl at school," Miles said. His mother took the rose and held it to her nose.

"You didn't spill the salsa yet?" his father muttered, slapping a slice on one of the plates he had taken down from the cabinet. "Also, is that rose plastic?"

Miles let his backpack straps slide from his shoulders, clasped his hands together. "This pizza and this rose, it's just to say I'm sorry."

"Stop apologizing and come dance with me," his mother said, reaching out for him. "You remember this, Miles. We danced all the time when you were little." Miles's mother jibed back and forth, her arms and legs moving in sync.

"When you weren't pissing your pants, or pissing the bed, or pissing me off," his father joked.

"Whatever." His mother swatted his father's words

away and set the rose on the couch. "Just follow me."

And from there, Miles and his mother danced and danced, his body dipping and dodging almost as if he were boxing. "Less culo, more waistline. Hip. Hip. Let your body do what it wants. It's telling you how it wants to move," his mother instructed. Until his father cut in.

"*Yo soy un hombre sincero, de donde crece la palma,*" Celia sang.

"Wepa!" Miles mother hooted, taking his father by the hand.

"See, son, after you spill the salsa, then you hit her with a spin move," his father boasted. "Works every time."

A few hours later, as Miles sat in his room doing his weekly sneaker clean—a toothbrush to the sole—there was a knock at his door. Miles figured this was when they would drop the hammer. His father was known for doing things like this. Waiting a full day, laughing and joking and acting like everything was fine before—*bam!* Grounded.

"Come in."

And just as he thought, it was his father. He closed the door behind him and leaned against it. "They're looking good, man," he said.

"Thanks."

"So, we need to talk." Miles sighed, but his sigh was cut short by his father's next words. "About tomorrow. I just wanted to check in with you, make sure you were still up for it. If you're not, that's totally fine."

"For the prison? Yeah, I'm up for it." Miles, relieved, set his shoe down. "You still up for it?"

Now Miles's father sighed. "Yeah." He came over to the bed, took a seat. "Let's just make sure that we're good with whatever happens. In case we find out he's not who we think he is. Or if he says something upsetting. Prison, it . . . does things to you. Trust me, I know." Miles could hear the discomfort in his father's voice, could hear his throat drying. But Miles didn't respond. Just looked at his dad and nodded. His father slapped his hands on his own thighs and rocked up from the bed. "Okay, that's all I wanted to say." He leaned down and kissed Miles on the forehead. "Good night."

As he opened the door, he turned back. "Oh, and thanks for the pizza." A sly grin wiped across his mug. "Though an anchovy or two would've been nice."

With the weight of the day heavy on Miles, sleep slipped into his room as his father slipped out. It wasn't long before Miles was overcome by it—dream state—and when it happened, it happened seamlessly. Miles didn't remember lying down, or snuggling in. Just sitting on his bed, then suddenly, as if in a blink, sitting on a couch. A leather couch. But not in his house. *That* house. The one Miles had never been to, but knew so well. The small window of his room, now palatial with off-white linen curtains snatched closed. His bare feet on mosaic tile floors. The smell of dirt, and wet, and tobacco smoke. Strands of cat hair floated through the air like tiny spirits.

"You know the issue I have with you, Miles?" The voice came from the seat beside him. He hadn't noticed anyone sitting there, despite how large the chair was. It was Mr. Chamberlain. All yellow and flimsy-skinned. All mustache and chapped lips. He sat with his hands together, his nails bitten down to the cuticles. "It's your arrogance. You believe that you can really save people. That you can do good. Superpowers don't belong to branches that come from a tree like yours. Because your tree is rotten at the roots. You, my man, are meant to be chopped down."

Miles couldn't speak. It was like his tongue had been cut from his mouth. In a panic, he slid to the far end of the couch, the leather grunting with each inch. Just then, a white cat pounced onto the backrest. Miles looked at it. Then back at Mr. Chamberlain, who had now become an even more ghostly figure. Long white hair hanging from his chin. Sharpened nose. Teeth like grilled corn kernels. "Spider-Man." The man spoke, his voice haunting, his smile disgusting. "You don't know me, but I know you. And I *will* come for you."

## CHAPTER NINE

**"Y**ou don't know *me*. I know *you!*" Miles's father yelled playfully down the hallway. Miles woke up, his heart beating like a wild animal trying to break free from his chest. "If you come, Rio, Miles is gonna come home with cuts in his eyebrows and parts all over the place."

"Ha! Jeff, this ain't the nineties. Kids aren't getting cuts in their eyebrows anymore."

"That's not the point. The point is, you would let the boy do whatever he wanted."

"Well, that's because it's his hair, papi."

"Yes, I know." *Knock, knock, knock.* "Miles, get up, man! We need to get you a haircut before we head up to the jail." Miles's father continued down the hall. "Yes, baby, I know. But he goes to that school, and I just don't want them saying nothing crazy about our boy. Let's just keep it clean until summer. Then I don't care if he shaves his eyebrows *off*!"

"Why you keep talking about eyebrows?"

*Good morning*, Miles said to himself, his hands covering his face as his eyes adjusted to the sun pouring in through his window. But one eye wouldn't open. He rubbed it and rubbed it until it watered, but the tears still didn't flush out whatever it was. He went to the bathroom; using two fingers to pull the skin around his eye in either direction, he used his other hand to pick out whatever was in his eye. He held it up in front of the mirror. A long white hair.

Which led to a long hot shower.

But not long enough before his mother was banging on the bathroom door.

"Miles, we have to pay for that hot water!" And "Miles, your father's getting impatient, and you know what that means!"

That meant that Miles's father would eat Miles's breakfast. Just out of spite.

Eventually, Miles shook off the strange nightmare, finished scalding his skin, got dressed, scarfed down breakfast—eggs and microwaved waffles—kissed his mother, watched his father kiss his mother, then set out on Saturday Mission #1: The Barbershop.


"Listen to what I'm saying to you."

"No, you listen to what I'm saying to *you*. I been comin' here since I was a kid, and now you got me paying thirty dollars for a daggone cut, House? A number one with a shave? Thirty *dollars*?"

"Well, that's fifteen for a cut, fifteen for a shave. Ten for kids. And eight for geniuses." House nodded at Miles.

"Uh-huh. Robbery." The complainer groaned.

"*Robbery?* You know what, y'all jokers kill me. Michael Jordan says, *today I've decided to charge three hundred smackers for my sneakers*, and y'all don't *never* have a problem buying those spaceships for shoes. Out here looking like your feet are in the future and the rest of your dusty butt is still in the hood. But the *one* minute"—House, the owner of House's Cut House, put a finger in the air—"the *one* minute I raise the price on haircuts, everybody whinin' and cryin'. Not to mention, ain't nobody getting their butts whipped over a fresh fade."

He was cutting the hair of a man dressed in construction clothes—dirty jeans and clay-caked boots. He ran the clippers over his head, hair rolling off in clumps, snowflaking to the floor.

"Look, I just feel like there's gotta be a loyalty discount." The man barking about the prices was sitting next to Miles and his father. He looked like one of those guys who was pushing fifty but played pick-up basketball with hack-boxes like Benji and Mucus Man every weekend to keep him young.

"*Loyalty?*" House turned the clippers off and pointed them at the man. "You don't know nothin' 'bout loyalty. If I don't charge you what I do, then I can't make the rent on this place. Are *you* gon' call me and invite me over to your *dee-lux* apartment in the sky for me to touch up your hairline and shave your face? You suckers talk all this trash like New York City ain't the new Disney World, and when was the last time Mickey Mouse offered you a free pass into that castle thing or whatever the hell they got down there? Huh? Never!"

"Man, just hurry up so the rest of us can get cut. Always talkin'."

"Oh, you gon' get cut, alright. Keep yappin'. Plus, you know the deal—you either wait or skate. You after Shorty Forty over there, anyway." House was talking about Miles. "Y'all know why I call him that, because he always gets a four-point-oh. One of the smartest people in the whole hood, and definitely the smartest in this barbershop."

Mr. Frankie, whose jeans were covered in paint splotches, was playing chess with Derrick, one of the younger barbers who didn't have any clients at this point in the day. He usually cut the little kids' hair because he knew how to do a funny helium-toned voice that always made them stop crying, and they didn't start coming in until around eleven. Ms. Shine was also in there. She had a mini bush and always came to House to get it trimmed down.

"My Cyrus was a four-point-oh student back in the day. The biggest nerd y'all ever wanted to meet," Ms. Shine said, a shaky sweetness to her voice. "Let that be a lesson to you, Miles—leave that dope alone."

"Yes, ma'am," Miles answered. Ms. Shine nodded and pinched her lips.

"Where's old Cyrus these days?" House asked. "Ain't seen him."

Ms. Shine stared blankly. "Me neither. A while ago the cops came to the house and took him away. I ain't heard from him since, but I figured he's better off in there than he was out here. At least in there he can maybe get some help. Get clean."

"Yeah," Miles father said. "I'm sure he's okay." Then silence. The discomfort seemed to lower the ceiling of the shop. Finally, House spoke up.

"You know who else I haven't seen? Backseat Benny."

"Who?" Ms. Shine snapped out of her trance of sadness.

"Benny. Homeless dude who sleeps in the car around the corner. He used to come here and I'd give him a cut in exchange for him sweeping up the hair."

"Oh yes. I didn't know that was his name. I used to leave coffee cans full of cookies on the trunk on Thanksgiving and Christmas. I haven't seen him."

"Me neither," Derrick said, moving his queen to the other side of the chessboard.

"I've seen him," Frankie said. "Maybe two weeks ago. He was getting yanked out of his car and thrown in the back of a paddy wagon."

"What he do?" House asked, swiping the smock from around the construction worker's neck and brushing the extra hair from his sweatshirt.

"I have no idea," Frankie said. "But that was the last time I saw him."

Miles thought of the poem he had written for Ms.

Blaufuss's class about Backseat Benny, "Disappearing Men." He'd been there for so long, yet so few people knew his name. Same went for Neek. He rarely left his house, so if you didn't live across the street from him, where you could see him peering through the blinds, you'd never know he was there. And Cyrus Shine was a zombie most days, ignored by most people. "Invisible Men" would've fit just as well.

The whole barbershop broke into a fit of head shaking, and afterward the conversation rolled on as usual. House sprayed sheen on the construction worker's hair, the smell of coconut and vanilla filling the air. Then House used his hand to lay the man's waves, before holding the mirror up in front of his face.

The man nodded. Paid. Tipped. And left.

"Shorty Forty, you up!" House said, slapping hair from the barber chair. As soon as Miles sat down, his father blurted out, "Low Caesar. A number one. Nothing special, please."

"Whoa. Relax, Jeff. Why you actin' like I ain't never cut his hair before? When he sit in my chair, you turn it off, and I turn it on," House said. "*Anyway*, how's school, Miles?"

"It's okay." *It sucks.*

"You figure out how to build a teleportation device yet?"

"I wish somebody would." Derrick moved knight to jump pawn.

"Nah, not yet," Miles said. "I'm just trying stay focused and get up out of there." *Also, I think my teacher might be trying to kill me.*

"I know that's right," the argumentative man next to him said. "I want House to stay focused because I'm trying to get up out of *here*!"

And on it went, the chatter about haircut prices, the gossip about how much so-and-so sold their house for, and how much the new house down south cost. The occasional pumping of the radio volume whenever one of House's jams came on, offbeat eighties tunes that were used for hip-hop samples, as Miles's father always liked to remind him. And the feeling of the plastic guard gliding over Miles's head, hair falling in his face, the hot blade on his neck, then on his forehead, and the familiar sound of the buzzing in his ear. When his cut was complete, Miles's father stood up to pay, but Miles pulled out what was left of his money from the ridiculous showtime moment on the train the day before.

"I got it," he said to his father, counting out the ones.

"Are you stripping, son?" House asked.

Derrick and the mad man both laughed. Ms. Shine turned away to hide her grin.

"No."

"Better not be," Miles's father added.

"I'm not." Miles slammed the money in House's palm. "But I do need a job. And since Benny is missing—uh, arrested—maybe I can come sweep up on Saturday."

House nodded, still holding Miles's hand, the money smashed between their palms. "What you charge?"

"Ten dollars an hour and free cuts for me and him."

House looked over at Miles's dad, who looked on, proud. "What are you, thirteen?"

Miles flashed to Mr. Chamberlain's class. Him on the floor at the broken desk.

*Thirteen.*

*Except as a punishment for crime* . . .

"Sixteen," Miles's father answered for him, jolting Miles back into the barbershop.

"I know, but he's brutal like a thirteen-year-old. My grandson's in the eighth grade, and he tries to hustle me every time I see him." House scratched his chin. "How 'bout this. Eight-fifty, and free cuts for *you*."

"Deal!" Miles's father jumped in again, unable to control himself. "He'll start next week."

"Great, glad we got that settled," the back-talker from earlier grumped. "Now can y'all please . . . *please* get out the way so this fool can cut my hair?"

Time for Saturday Mission #2: Visiting Austin.

The ride to the prison consisted mostly of Miles's father talking loudly over early nineties rap music about how happy he was to see him "take some initiative" and ask House for a job, and how he and his brother started trying to make money for themselves at Miles's age too, but that they did it illegally. Meanwhile, Miles was texting Ganke.

**11:51am** to Ganke
YO YOU MADE IT THRU DINNER OK?

**11:52am** 1 New Message from Ganke
IM STILL ALIVE. NO TEARS

"If only we were as smart as you, Miles. Nothing wrong with making money slow, son. Always remember that," Miles's father said.

**11:54am** to Ganke
COOL. HEADED TO THE JAIL NOW

"You hear me, Miles? You listening?" his father asked.
"Yes. I hear you. Money, slow," Miles said.

**11:55am** 1 New Message from Ganke
NEVER EVER TEXT THAT AGAIN! IT'S LIKE A JINX OR SOMETHIN

Miles leaned forward and knocked on the wood paneling that lined the dashboard in his dad's car. He wasn't sure it meant anything or that it would do anything, and he even felt a little stupid about it, but just in case. Knock on wood.

Almost an hour later, the car bumped onto Old Factory Road in the most barren part of Brooklyn Miles had ever seen. Lots of land. No big buildings. Well, one big building. They pulled up to the prison and were greeted by a big cement sign. DEPARTMENT OF CORRECTIONS. Guards stood post outside the giant windowless block. There were cranes and bulldozers, cones and tape, on one side of the building.

"This place is always under construction. Shoot, I think they were working on it way back when me and Aaron used to pop in and out of here," Miles's father explained. "It was much smaller back then." He killed the engine. Miles couldn't stop fidgeting, and he tried to calm himself down. "Before we go in here, I need to reiterate that prison changes people. So I don't want you to have high expectations or anything like that. Let's just meet him where he is." Miles nodded and reached for his door handle. "And also," his father continued. Miles paused in the middle of opening his door. "I know I mentioned this before, but I just need you to know that whatever happens, if he's related to us or not, I'm proud of you for wanting to come see him. Y'know, me and Aaron sat in the juvie ward with no visitors. Our mother couldn't bear seeing us in jail, and our father was . . . y'know." Miles nodded, pushed his door open. "So . . . I'm proud of you for caring," his dad finished.

After walking through the metal detector and being scanned by a man the size *of* a metal detector, Miles and his father moved through the sterile check-in room to the clerk.

"Who you here to see?" she asked through a small window.

"Austin Davis."

"Sign in, and ID, please."

Miles and his father signed the clipboard perched on the ledge in front of the window. Visitor Name. Visited Name. Date. Time In. Miles's father slid his ID through the window. The lady made a copy and handed it back.

"Okay, Mr. Davis. Somebody will be out to get y'all in a second."

"Um, sorry, but this is visiting time, right?" Miles's father asked, looking around the empty room.

"Yes it is, sir."

"Where is everybody else?"

The lady behind the desk shook her head. "Looks like you're it."

Miles watched as his father looked around the gray room of nothing again. It was like he was examining the corners, the cameras, remembering what it felt like to be there. Miles wondered if his father was thinking about his brother going in and out long after he'd given up the life. That his brother didn't have any visitors because he wouldn't come.

On the ashen walls were three frames of signage aligned like expensive abstract art in a gallery. Miles took a closer look. The first, in bold black letters above a sheriff star, read:

KINGS COUNTY DEPARTMENT OF CORRECTIONS
IMPORTANT NOTICE
VISITATION SCHEDULE
SATURDAYS: LAST NAMES STARTING WITH
   LETTERS A–L
SUNDAYS: LAST NAMES STARTING WITH LETTERS M–Z

The next one was a layout of the rules.

**PARENTS**
- Visitors who appear intoxicated may be denied access to visitation
- Visitors who are inappropriately dressed (sexually or gang affiliated) may be denied access to visitation
- Parents must stay with their other visiting children at all times
- No styling or braiding of youth's hair in the visiting room

As Miles read on, his father walked up beside him and joined him in reading the long list of rules.

**YOUTH**
- Youth are not to shake hands with any youth in the visiting area
- No swearing
- Zero gang tolerance
- Dress appropriately. No slippers, and pants pulled up to waist.
- No passing of letters, phone numbers, or mail
- No loud talk

Finally, a startling buzz, like an electrocution. Then another. Then a door opened, and a guard stepped in.

"Davis?" she said, her voice bouncing off the walls of the empty waiting area. "This way, please."

Miles and his dad went through the door, only to stop

and wait for it to close completely before the next door opened. The clinking of the dead bolt jamming locked, matched with the scraping of the next door's lock pulling back, sent a chill down Miles's spine. Once the second door was open, they walked down the corridor, which strangely reminded Miles of the halls of his middle school. There was nothing but the sticky sound of rubber rolling off linoleum, and an occasional squeak.

And before they knew it, Miles and his father were there. At the door to the visiting room. The guard pushed a buzzer and waited. A buzz came loud through a small speaker in the call box, followed by the dead bolt retracting. The guard swung the door open, entered first, then gestured for Miles and his father to join.

It was an empty room. Big enough for at least twenty people, and furnished with enough seating for that amount. But there was only one person there, besides another guard who was posted up against the wall. Miles guessed that guard's job was to escort Austin from his cell to the room, and back. There was a boy sitting at one table, a matted Afro, khaki uniform, his hands nervously tapping on the table. The skin on his face sagged with exhaustion, making him look older than he was. The guard who had escorted Miles and his father spoke to the other guard, then stood in the opposite corner.

"Austin?" Miles's father called out, walking toward him, Miles right beside him. Miles's father extended his hand.

"No touching," Austin's escort snapped.

"That's right." Miles's dad pulled his hand back, glancing back at the guard. "I forgot." He and Miles sat down at the small table.

"Um . . ." Austin started. "What do I call you?"

Miles just stared at Austin, at his face.

"I . . . Look, that's not important. Uh . . . this is Miles." Austin looked at Miles. "Wassup, man."

"Wassup," Miles said back, studying Austin's eyes. He wasn't looking for a tell, a break in some sort of disguise that would let him know that Austin wasn't who he said he was. Miles knew Austin was exactly who he said he was—that he was family. He knew it from the moment he entered the room.

A balloon of awkwardness inflated around them. "So, you're Uncle Aaron's son, huh?" Miles asked, trying to burst it.

"Yeah."

Miles's dad brushed his hand down his face. "Can you just . . . explain it to me? I just . . ."

"You just didn't know I existed. I know," Austin said, blunt. "Look, we don't have a lot of time in here, and y'all don't gotta stay if you don't want. I just wanted someone else to know I was here. Someone else that was blood. My grandma too old to be coming up here."

"Okay, so, my brother was your father," Miles's father said. "But who's your mother?"

"Her name was Nadine."

Miles watched his father roll that name around his brain, trying to place it. "Nadine? I don't remember a Nadine."

"Yeah, she and my father weren't together but they stayed close, y'know."

"And she's . . ." Miles said.

"She's dead."

"Sorry to hear that."

"Yeah, me too. She was the best. You know how some people are so easy to love you'd just do anything for them? That's how she was."

"Yeah," Miles said, thinking of his own mother. There was a pause, a moment where everyone sized each other up.

"Look, kid . . . Austin, why are we here?" Miles's father asked, his voice pushy.

"I told you."

"But what do you want from me? From us?"

Austin leaned back in his chair. "I don't want nothin'. Ain't nothin' you can give me. Except . . ." Austin leaned forward again. "Tell me why you ain't never come around?"

Miles's father hmph'd. "Because me and your father didn't get along."

"So you just cut him off for almost twenty years?"

"I had to. I don't know how much you know about Aaron, but . . ."

"I know what he was into."

"Well, then, it should make sense that I had to leave Aaron alone after I decided to get out the game and realized he couldn't. Or should I say, he wouldn't."

"But he did."

"What?"

Austin smirked, nodded. "He did give it up. For a

while." Austin looked at Miles. "Did you know him?" Miles looked at his father and thought about all the secret visits he had made to his uncle's house without his parents knowing. He thought about the pizza and the grape soda, the grimy apartment in the Baruch projects. He thought about the last time he saw him, the battle, the explosion.

"Kinda, but not really," Miles said, scratching the spider bite on the top of his hand.

"Well, he was cool," Austin said, regaining Miles's attention. "A good dude, who wanted to do right by people, but just . . . I don't know. I mean, when my mother was pregnant with me, my pops decided he was gonna be a family man."

"That don't sound like Aaron," Miles's father said.

"Well, it was. My mother always said he watched how you straightened up once you got married and started a family and all that, and he felt like that was what he needed to do, too. And he did. Got a regular job making dough at a pizza spot. And even though that wasn't a whole bunch of money, it was enough to add to the pot with my moms to keep a roof over our head. But then she got sick."

"Your mom?" Miles asked.

"Yeah. Stomach cancer. Had to stop working and all that. And after a while, the money ran out. I don't know how much chemo and all that cost, but I know it's a lot. So, my pops went back to the basics."

"Robbery."

Austin winced a little when Miles said it. "Yeah. Everything he got he sold for money to pay her doctor bills. At least, almost everything. He always kept a little to the side to buy me sneakers, which was cool. But, y'know, then . . . he died."

Miles readjusted in his seat, discomfort clinging to him like wet cotton.

"So I picked up the slack. Tried to lift that burden. Couldn't just let my mother waste away without at least trying. I cut back on school—wasn't doing so great anyway, and teachers never seemed to bother to ask why—and figured stealing cars as a minor would be a slap on the wrist if I got caught. But when I did, they trumped my charges when they found out who my father was. So now I'm in here. Been in here for almost a year. And I can deal with it most days, but there are a few things that are hard to shake, and one of them is the fact that my mother passed away the day I came in."

That was another punch in the gut for Miles, and as he glanced at his now-softening father, Miles figured this phantom fist of guilt had taken the air out of him too.

"I'm so sorry to hear that, Austin."

"Me too," Miles said.

"Yeah, me too." Austin forced a sad smirk. Miles had grown used to that painful smile because Ganke did it often.

"Five minutes," the guard called out, her voice bouncing off the cold walls. Miles looked back at her, then turned to Austin.

"Um, what are some other things that are hard to shake?" Miles asked.

"What?" Austin squinted.

"Miles." Miles could feel his father's glare on the side of his face. He ignored him and continued.

"You said there were a few things that were hard to shake. One being your . . . um . . . mother." Miles swallowed. "But . . . what else?"

"You don't have to answer that." Miles's father cocked his head to the side and looked at his son like he had lost his mind. "What are you thinking?"

Miles didn't know how to answer that. Because he didn't really have an answer. He just knew that he was looking in the face of someone who looked just like him. Who, for whatever reason, did what he thought he had to do, just like him. Who loved his family despite their flaws, just like him.

"It's okay." Austin leaned forward, knit his fingers together, looked Miles in the face. "Sometimes, I have nightmares. Been having them on and off for years. But since I've been in here, they've been worse."

Now, Miles leaned in. His father, however, leaned back. "What kind of nightmares?" Miles asked.

"Just crazy stuff. I mean, look, everybody locked up in here comes from similar situations as mine. Either forced to act a certain way to survive, or totally forgotten about. And they all look like me—like us—too, if you know what I mean. So, sometimes in my dreams, everybody in this place changes. Like they all turn into things, everybody but me. And they attack me. So when I wake up, I be looking at them crazy. Because my dreams have me thinking I can't trust nobody in here. Then, other times, it's just simple stuff, baby nightmares." He lowered his voice and continued. "Like that jerk over there telling me I ain't never gon' be nothing. Which ain't really much of a nightmare, because he always says that when I'm awake. Only difference is, in my dream, he got my daddy's voice."

"Jesus . . ." Miles's father shook his head, visibly upset.

"You're just like me," Austin said.

"What?" Miles backed away a bit.

"That's what he always says in the dream. 'You're just like me.' "

"Time!" the guard yelled out.

Miles and his father stood up. Miles, jumpy from what he'd just heard, almost extended his hand for a five but remembered contact wasn't allowed.

"Ah. I feel like we were just getting to know each other. Well, if y'all don't come back, it's cool. Thanks for at least coming this time," Austin said, unable to hide his disappointment.

"Wait, one last question," Miles said.

"We have to go." His father tapped him on the arm.

"I know, but this will be quick. What do all the other guys in here turn into in your dreams?"

Miles's father turned around to let the guard know that they'd heard her. All of Brooklyn had heard her.

Austin looked puzzled by the question. "I don't know, white cats and crazy stuff like that."

"White cats?" Miles repeated, as his father, now gripping his arm, turned him around.

"Yeah, why?"

"We'll . . . um . . . come back to see you," Miles's father struggled to get out, cutting the conversation before they were barked at again by the guard. "We will." And as they walked across the room, Miles turned to eyeball the officer coming to escort Austin back to his cell. His badge glinted under the fluorescent light. His name tag wasn't big enough for most people to see from where they were, but Miles could see it clearly. CHAMBERLAIN.

Miles glanced over at his father every few minutes on the car ride home. His dad's eyes were focused on the road, but there were lines like canals that dug into his forehead. Miles hoped his father wasn't thinking about the whole white cat thing, because there was no way Miles could explain it all yet. He didn't really understand it all himself. There was so much on Miles's mind that he felt physically heavy, as if the bones in his body were suddenly denser. White cats, and his teacher, and the nightmares he had been having about his uncle. His uncle. The sneakers that were always in his uncle's house made more sense now.

"So . . ." Miles's father said, the wrinkles in his head relaxing as they finally pulled up in front of their house. He put the car in park. "That was . . . interesting."

"Yeah," Miles said, not sure what else to say about it all.

"I just . . . I never knew. I know that when you make

decisions you have to live with them, y'know, but I never thought about why he may have been doing some of the things he did. Or even what bumped him off the track, even though I was there when it happened. I just wish I would've reached out to him. Maybe tried to figure out a way to help him out. Shoot, I might've even been able to get him a job," Miles's father said. "But I thought he was still dirty. Like, I always thought he just couldn't help himself. Or . . . didn't want to. Like he'd ruined his name to the point of no return, and all I wanted was to be left alone."

*All we ask is to be let alone.* The Jefferson Davis quote from class flashed across Miles's mind like a lightning bolt to the brain. Miles looked at his father, could see the struggle in his eyes, could hear the lump moving in his throat. "There's always more to the story, right? I mean, a name, whether good or bad, is almost never *just* a name. There's always something behind it. Something more to it."

"Yeah. I guess you're right," his father said. "Maybe next weekend we can pop back in there, check him out, if you're up to it. After your job, of course." A proud smile appeared on Miles's father's face. "Plus, you know your mother's gonna want to meet him."

They climbed out of the car and made their way upstairs. When Miles opened the door, Ganke and Miles's mom were sitting on the couch watching an all-Spanish-speaking television channel.

"Wait, Mrs. M. What did she just say?" Ganke asked.

Miles's mother was sitting on the couch next to him, plucking grapes from a plastic bag.

"She said she loves him."

"But you said she said she loved him a few seconds ago."

"Because she did, Ganke."

"Hmm. Okay, well what's he saying?"

"He's saying he's dying."

"Um . . . hello?" Miles said.

"Hey, Miles," Ganke threw over his shoulder.

"Ay, mijo, you look like my son again," Miles's mother teased. Miles's father bent over the couch and kissed her on the top of her head. "How was . . . everything?"

"In one day our son has been to jail and got a job," Miles's father quipped.

"I didn't know you were coming over here this early, man," Miles said to Ganke, ignoring his parents. He sat on the arm of the sofa.

"Neither did I," Miles's father said.

"Me either, but you better be glad you aren't on punishment or I would've had to send him all the way back home."

That was the first time since he'd been home that Miles knew for sure he wasn't on punishment. He crushed his smile between his jaws, but inside, he was so, so happy. No more ramen noodles for him.

"Of *course* I was coming over." Ganke kept one eye and one ear on the television. "We've got work to do."

"Work?" Miles asked.

"Work?" his mother echoed before being sucked back into the TV love affair.

"Halloween costumes and stuff like that," Ganke nudged, bouncing his brows.

"Yeah, Halloween costumes. For the party. At the school," Miles added, not nearly as smoothly.

"Are you trying to ask me something, Miles Morales?" his mother said. His father blew a raspberry.

"You didn't ask them?" Ganke squealed.

"Um . . . Ma, tonight's the school Halloween party." Miles showed his teeth. "And Ganke's going."

Miles's father blew another raspberry. "Boy, just say you wanna go!"

Miles's mother rotated back and forth between soap opera and son, pausing on Miles.

"Ma, can I please go?"

"Is the girl going to be there?"

"Ma."

"What? I'm just asking!" She turned to Ganke. "Is she, Ganke?"

"I think so," Ganke replied, that devilish look in his eye.

"Uh-huh. Well, I guess you can go," she said, smirking, and turned back to the TV.

In Miles's room, Ganke collapsed on Miles's bed, while Miles took the floor.

"So, you made it through the dinner, I see."

"Yeah. It wasn't too bad. Like I put in the text, there was no crying. But that's because we decided to eat while watching one of those crime shows where it's like a real case but they haven't solved it yet. Cops found out this dude's wife had him ground up in one of those tree grinders. It was gross. But . . . entertaining."

"Wow."

"Right," Ganke said. "What about you? How was meeting your cousin? Uh . . . cousin, right?"

"Yeah, cousin. It was weird, man. But good. He looks just like me, which was a trip. We didn't get a lot of time to talk because my dad was hogging most of the questions, but the one thing I found out is that he's been having the same nightmares as me. Oh, and the crazy, *crazy* thing was that the guard monitoring him was named Chamberlain. It was on his badge."

"Did he look like a troll that, if provoked, might grind people up in a tree-grinding machine?"

"What?" Miles stood, walked over to the closet.

"Not important. Anyway, are y'all gonna go back?"

"I think so. I mean, the way I see it, we kinda have to. Austin's on lockdown."

"Yeah." Ganke nibbled on a fingernail. "You know who's *not* on lockdown? You. No punishment. I don't even know how you pulled that off."

"Yeah, me neither." Miles inspected his haircut in the mirror hanging on the back of his closet door. "The school didn't call about the desk, and other than that, I just told my dad the whole story about leaving the store and Alicia, and he told my mother everything, and I guess that smoothed things out."

"Alicia, who's probably going to come to the party tonight looking like some kind of gorgeous ghoul. Too bad you'll be a ghost to her."

"Nah." Miles turned to Ganke. "I'm gonna spill the salsa on her."

"Wait, you're gonna do what?"

"Don't worry about it."

"Well, listen, being such a positive figure in your life, I pretty much willed you out of trouble and knew that you wouldn't be prepared for freedom, so I brought you one of my old costumes." Ganke reached into his backpack and pulled out a plastic bag. In it was a rubber mask. He handed it to Miles.

"What is it?"

"A zombie," Ganke explained. "And the best part is, you can dress the way you've been dressing for the last few days and it'll work perfectly. You're already eighty-five percent there!" Ganke flashed a goofy face.

After running scenarios of what might happen when Miles finally decided to approach Alicia and talking a lot about salsa, both "spilling it" and dancing it, it was time to get dressed for the party. Miles threw on raggedy sweats, an old T-shirt, and the zombie mask. It wasn't amazing, but it was good enough. Ganke, on the other hand, put on a wool suit, a pink swim cap, and little circle-framed glasses.

"Who are you supposed to be, man?" Miles asked, sizing Ganke up.

"I'm Dean Kushner, pretending to be Mr. Chamberlain,"

he said, putting his hands together and closing his eyes. "I'm literally going to stand in the middle of the dance floor like this the whole time."

Miles howled with laughter.

"Miles!" his mother's voice came from down the hall. Miles cracked the door.

"Yes!"

"Come speak to everybody. John John and the guys are here."

John John was a former Marine and lawyer who was one of Miles's father's closest friends. He and "the guys" Miles's mother was talking about were in the living room, same as they were one Saturday a month for as long as Miles could remember. Playing cards. Spades, to be exact.

By the time Miles and Ganke were headed out—about ten minutes after the announcement of John John—the spades crew was settled in the living room, and the game was in full swing.

"Punks jump up to get beat down!" Carlo, an old friend of Miles's father from his previous life as a street guy, taunted. Carlo was always dressed in a button-down shirt and hard-bottom shoes and had a scar on his cheek that looked like a millipede. He was holding a card in the air, waiting for Miles's father to play his hand. Miles's dad laid a queen of clubs down, and Carlo slapped a five of spades on top of it. "Get that mess outta here, boy!" Carlo jeered, raking up the cards.

Next to him was Sherman. Everybody called him Sip because he was from Mississippi. He didn't talk too much.

Miles's father met Sip the same night he met Rio, at that Super Bowl party. When Miles's father asked him why he left Mississippi, all he said was, "The dust got too thick." Miles's father didn't know exactly what that meant, but he knew it had nothing to do with dust.

"Uh-huh," Sip grunted, cutting the cards. "You boys get happy so quickly up here in New York. Sometimes things gotta get warm before they get hot."

"Sip, please," John John said, tapping the cards. "You been living here almost twenty years. You one of us now."

"No I ain't. I'm a crooked-letter boy to the grave. A city-dweller now, for sure, but trust me, I still know the ways of the South. Still understand patience." Sip winked at Miles's father, his spades partner. John John shook his head and started dealing.

Miles and Ganke walked into the kitchen for a quick glass of juice before leaving.

"Oh!" Miles's mother, who had been at the counter shaking trick-or-treat candy into a bowl, shrieked. "You babies look so cute!"

"Ain't no babies in this house!" Carlo yelled from the living room.

"They are to her," Miles's father said under his breath.

"They are to me!" Miles's mother yelled back. "Take a look," she said, presenting Miles and Ganke to the older men at the card table.

"And who you supposed to be, son?" Miles's father asked. Miles wasn't wearing his mask.

"A zombie." Miles flung the mask in the air.

"Well, guess what," John John said. "You nailed it."

"Sure did," Sip followed up with some additional snark while rearranging the cards in his hand.

"And what about you, Ganke?" Miles's father asked.

"It's complicated. But basically, I'm me and Miles's dean, pretending to be our history teacher, Mr. Chamberlain."

Miles's mother let out a high-pitched squeal. "That's funny. But I'm glad it was you and not Miles who tried to pull this stunt."

"Yeah. He would've been suspended, again." Miles's father shook his head.

"Kiddo got suspended?" John John laid his cards on the table, facedown, and took a swig of his drink.

"Yeah, his teacher Mr. Chamberlain wrote him up for running out of class for a, um, bathroom emergency."

"And they *suspended* him for that? Because the kid had to go, what, one . . . or two?" Carlo added.

"Doesn't matter. That seems a bit excessive with the discipline, even to me," John John said.

"Man, lemme tell you something, I ain't never met a Chamberlain I liked," Carlo said, also putting his cards down. "Matter fact, when I was in school, I struggled with a teacher named Mr. Chamberlain too."

"Did he look like this?" Ganke asked, instantly taking on his Chamberlain pose—hands together, eyes closed.

"Um . . . nah." Carlo peered at Ganke. "This dude had a weird red bush. Like Ronald McDonald. And he wasn't my history teacher. He was my English teacher. But

I wasn't a good reader, you know. And he knew that. But he would call on me anyway. Every single day."

"Did you tell him you didn't want to read?" Miles asked.

"Yeah, I told him. I even stayed after class one day and explained that I maybe needed a tutor or something. But he didn't care. He just kept calling on me, letting the other kids laugh at me, until one day I just started ignoring him. And when *that* happened, he started writing me up. And it wasn't long before I wasn't in school no more at all."

Miles's father shook his head. "And how old were you?"

"I don't know. Probably fifteen or sixteen. Old enough to put my hands in the poison pot, which you *know* I did." He nodded at Miles's father.

"Funny," Sip grumbled. "I had a Mr. Chamberlain too. Except he wasn't no teacher. He was Principal Chamberlain, but we always called him Old Man Chamberlain. He was a Mississippi good ol' boy who ain't give two shakes about kids like me." Sip cracked the knuckles in his hands. "One day I got into a scuffle with a kid named Willie Richards for calling me out by name. Now, everybody saw it in the lunchroom. Willie said what he said. And I let it roll off me like water on a duck's back. He was just mad about me being better than him on the football field. Stupid. But then dirtbag had the nerve to spit on me, and well, ain't no coming back from being spat on. So, I . . . well . . . let's just say Willie, wherever he is right now, is probably still wishing he coulda sucked that spit back in his mouth." The guys at the table all laughed. Ganke and Miles did too. "Old Man Chamberlain didn't find it funny though, nor did he think I was justified. So he expelled me. He was always kicking black kids out, though, so it really wasn't no big surprise."

"Did you go to a different school?" Miles asked.

"I tried. But when you got what I had on my record, and you living in Mississippi back then, ain't nobody wanna be bothered with you. I was gonna go to college. Get my mother out that old clapboard house. But that required money, and I just felt so . . . I don't know . . . like I couldn't win for losing. And guess what? When the world is breaking your back, it get a whole lot easier to break some laws."

"Ain't that the truth," Carlo said.

And the Chamberlain stories continued. John John, the only person at the table who hadn't dabbled in crime, had also been given the blues by a Mr. Chamberlain.

"I mean, I had a lot of tough teachers. But the one that gave it to me the worst, funny enough, was also named . . . Chamberlain."

"Yeah, I remember," Miles's father said. He and Aaron had gone to school with John John. "He used to ride Aaron hard."

"That's right. What was his actual title, again? Because he wasn't really a teacher."

"He was the dean of discipline. He literally used to just walk the halls, or pop into classrooms and pick out students he felt needed to be chastised. It just so happened that me, you, Aaron, and a few others were always those students."

"Yeah, like Tommy Rice. Remember him? Chamberlain

yanked him out of . . . I can't remember the teacher's name, but she taught social studies. Tommy was asleep, but the reason why is because Tommy was up all night looking after his little brothers and sisters because his mom was messed up, and he was *still* doing his homework and stuff. We all knew that. I think most of the teachers even knew that. But Chamberlain suspended him for sleeping. *Sleeping.* Said he was being nonverbally disrespectful."

"Yeah, he got Aaron on something crazy like that, too. Got him three times, and on the third he booted him from the school. But I kept going until Aaron started pulling up to the schoolyard in fancy cars."

"Other people's fancy cars," Miles's mother clarified, setting the bowl of candy on a small table by the front door.

"Right." The men all sat in silence for a moment.

"So the moral to the story is, don't trust nobody named Chamberlain unless it's Wilt Chamberlain. Got it?" Carlo gruffed.

"Oh, be quiet," Miles's mother said, wrapping her arms around Miles's and Ganke's shoulders. "There's no way you can blame all the bad stuff in your life on a few tough teachers."

"Absolutely not," Sip said. "I don't blame nobody for my life but me. But I'll tell you what, for some of us, school is like a tree we get to hide in. And at the bottom of it is a bunch of dogs. Them dogs are bad decisions. So when people shake us out that tree for no reason, it becomes a lot easier to get bit."

"And that there's the truth," John John agreed. "It don't always happen that way, but it definitely does happen."

"Don't matter what kind of family you from either. There's enough out here to snatch you away from a good upbringing, especially if you got idle time and no clear path to success. Man . . . forget about it," Carlo added.

"Okay, okay, that's enough." Miles's mother cut the conversation. "You boys leave these old men here to reminisce and complain while y'all go party." She gave Ganke a hug. And then she gave Miles one, and whispered in his ear, "Spill the salsa."

"How weird is it that all my dad's friends have bad stories about teachers named Mr. Chamberlain?" Miles asked Ganke as they walked to the train. He couldn't help but think about how one of the things that led them down the wrong road was being kicked out of school. School might've been the formula to create a continual function, a life drawn without interruption. Calculus. Or to Miles's father and his friends, basic arithmetic.

It was a strangely warm night for Halloween. Little kids dressed as witches and princesses, animals and Super Heroes, were all out, walking slowly up and down the block.

"I mean, it's weird, but no more weird than if we were to ask how many people had a bad teacher named Mr. Johnson," Ganke said. "It'd probably be like a million people. It's just one of those things. Besides, they were all different people. It would've been more of a shock if they all had the *same* Mr. Chamberlain, even the guy in Mississippi. Like our Mr. Chamberlain has spent his whole life as a *traveling* educational jerk."

"Word," Miles agreed, but it was still pinballing around his mind until they got to the train. The train was full of people, some dressed in extravagant costumes, others in simple masks, and some just trying to avoid the madness of Halloween. "But what about the guard?"

"Who?"

"The guard in the prison. The one I told you whose name was Chamberlain, too."

"Hmm. Co-winky-dink?"

Miles gnawed on his bottom lip as the train doors closed. "Doubt it."

Once they were back on the Brooklyn Visions Academy campus, the boys ran up to their room to drop off their backpacks, wipe the sweat from their necks, and reapply deodorant. Well, Miles did. Ganke reminded him about Koreans not having body odor.

"But I can smell you, dude," Miles said, digging around in his everyday jeans at the back of his closet. He pulled out the poem he had written Alicia—right where he'd left it. The denim had stained the paper indigo blue. Miles slipped it into his sweatpants, then checked himself out in the mirror. Such a shame his fresh haircut was going to be hidden under the zombie mask, Miles thought.

"That's *you* you smell, salsa boy," Ganke insisted. "Now, can we *please* get to the party? I got some standing in the middle of the floor to do."

They could hear the music blaring from the outside when they got to the party, a splattering of teenagers pushing through the double doors to join. The auditorium was packed with dancing students dressed in kooky costumes, some as elaborate as C-3PO, the golden robot from *Star Wars*, and others as simple as whiskers drawn on a face. The side walls were lined with tables of food and drinks, and up on the stage was Judge, dressed as a judge with a fat pair of headphones on his head, standing behind two turntables.

"First let's do a walk-through," Ganke screamed in Miles's ear. The two of them wormed through the crowd, trying to see who was there, and who wasn't. They recognized Winnie first because she was dressed in regular clothes—a sleeveless dress and heels. Miles asked her who she was supposed to be.

"What?!" she yelled back.

"Who are you?!" Miles leaned in closer.

"Oh. Michelle Obama!" she said, pointing to a small American-flag pin on her chest. The triplets, Sandy, Mandy, and Brandy, were dressed as the sun, moon, and stars, which were basically hokey costumes made from felt and an overused glue gun. Of course Ryan was there. Miles was expecting him to be dressed in something cheesy like a three-piece suit, but he was a shoddily crafted monster, which technically made him a good-looking monster. But then he opened his mouth and there were fangs. Of course. Any way to work in sucking on some girl's neck. There were teachers there as well, some dressed in costumes, and some not. Mrs. Khalil had elaborate feathered-wing attachments connected to her arms and a beak over her nose. It was enough of a costume for her to look cool but still be able to walk around and monitor the students, who were constantly looking over their shoulders for a chance to grind against one another. Ms. Blaufuss, on the other hand, went all out—Edgar Allan Poe. The jet-black hair, the stark white face, the black suit, and a stuffed raven perched on her arm the whole time. Nailed. It. Mrs. Tripley was dressed not as Frankenstein, but as Mary Shelley, the lady who *wrote* Frankenstein. As if anyone could tell. And Mr. Chamberlain was there too, as expected, dressed as a Civil War Confederate soldier, ghosting through the crowd, slipping in between dancing couples, wagging fingers.

When Miles and Ganke saw him coming toward them, Ganke stopped cold, put his hands together, and froze in Chamberlain-pose.

Miles, however, rushed out of the crowd. He didn't want to have any brush-ups with his teacher. At least not yet. He walked over to the punch table to pour himself a cup, but there was a line. The . . . thing waiting in front of him had a hunchback and a mess of matted hair. And smelled of sandalwood.

"Alicia?"

The ogre turned around, and sure enough it was her, her brown skin painted an awful green. She was ladling red juice into a red cup.

Alicia looked at Miles, but didn't say anything.

"Oh," he said, realizing he had his mask on, which also muffled his voice. "It's me." He yanked it up over his face.

"Oh, hey," she said, her tone sizzling with awkwardness as she dropped the scoop back in the bowl and stepped to the side. She opened her mouth as if she wanted to say something, but didn't.

*First pour a drink. Then, spill the salsa,* Miles reminded himself.

But before he could execute his plan, Alicia had ducked back into the crowd.

"Pour me one, bro," Ganke said just then, coming up on Miles's side. He took the full cup from Miles's hand, pounded it back.

"It's like she didn't even notice me."

"Oh yes she did. She was blushing!"

"Her face is gree—"

Before Miles could finish Ganke shouted, "But *he* didn't even notice *me*! Everybody else knew exactly what I was doing, but Chamberlain is so oblivious it's like he didn't even see me. Such a weirdo!"

Miles looked over Ganke's shoulder, scanning the room for where Alicia might've gone. He spotted her mixing into the mob of costumes.

"We'll talk about it later," Miles said, dashing off toward her. He burrowed through the crowd, trying his best to avoid bumping anybody and splashing juice all over the place. Not that it would've mattered. If anything, it would've just looked like more fake blood.

Miles, still unmasked, found Alicia in the center, huddled with some other people Miles recognized. At least the ones who weren't wearing masks. Most of them were her Dream Defender friends, like Dawn Leary, but others were students from class, like Brad Canby, dressed as a professional tennis player.

"Alicia!" Miles tried to get her attention, but she didn't hear him. He had been waiting for this moment all day, planning out in his head how he was going to do it, to say it. He slipped the folded poem out of his pocket. "Alicia!" She turned away from Dawn. "I have to tell you something!" Miles took a step toward her. As soon as he did, a volcano erupted in his stomach, an earthquake in his head. *Oh no.* And before he could say another word, Mr. Chamberlain came out of nowhere, wedging himself between Miles and Alicia. He eyeballed Miles. Miles swallowed hard.

"How about a little distance between you two, Morales. If I see you try anything inappropriate, we'll have a problem."

"Nobody's trying anything!" Alicia puffed up.

Miles's skin got hot, as if he were cooking from the inside out. But he held his tongue and nodded his head. Mr. Chamberlain walked away, pushing through the teenage jumble.

"Such a jerk," Alicia muttered. "And by the way, I have to tell you something, too. I'm sorry about what happened in class. I should've said something or . . . done something."

"It's, um . . . it's fine." Miles was distracted.

"Okay, well, there's something else I need to talk to you about, but first, what did you have to say?" Alicia asked, her face, though green, still pleasant.

"Huh?"

"What did you have to tell me?" she asked again, still bobbing her head to the music. She gave him a slight smile, her tongue resting gently between her teeth. But Miles was too busy darting his eyes at Mr. Chamberlain's back as he scolded other kids. He no longer felt the buzzing in his head that he was now certain was coming from Chamberlain, though the buzzing in his stomach, the one from Alicia, was still there. He thought about what his mother said when they were dancing in the living room. *Let your body do what it wants. It's telling you how it wants to move.*

"Uh . . ." Miles held the paper up, unfolded it. He watched as Mr. Chamberlain spoke to another teacher, tapped his watch like it was already time for him to go. "I just . . ." Miles turned back to Alicia, whose smile was slowly straightening, her head slightly tilted, her eyes ready to roll. Miles checked Mr. Chamberlain again as he headed for the side door, pushed it open. "I wanted to say . . ." Now Miles's attention was back on Alicia again. But only for a moment. Then, Chamberlain. Alicia. Chamberlain. Alicia. "Um, this is for you." Miles finally handed her the blue-stained paper with the sijo scribbled on it. Alicia, befuddled, began reading it, but by the time she lifted her eyes again, Miles was gone.

## CHAPTER TEN

**M**iles put the zombie mask back on before slipping out the side exit, which led outdoors. He looked to his left, then to his right, before activating camouflage mode. Then he slinked behind Mr. Chamberlain, who walked along the side of the school. He could hear Mr. Chamberlain's legs pumping like machine pistons, and matched his pace so Chamberlain couldn't hear the second set of feet walking with him. Mr. Chamberlain stopped at another door on the far side of the auditorium. He bent down, rolled up his pant legs, then pulled out a set of keys. He flipped through them until he found the right one, pushed it into the keyhole, and yanked the door open. Miles climbed up on the wall and scampered in through the quickly narrowing gap.

Mr. Chamberlain turned on a key-chain flashlight, a

single white beam shooting out in front of him like a laser. He whipped it left and right just to survey whatever was in front of him. Miles, still clinging to the wall, crept closer to get a better view. Stairs leading down. Mr. Chamberlain stepped lightly, his shoes clicking on each step as he descended into what seemed to be some kind of dark cellar.

But it wasn't a room at all. It was a tunnel. Miles knew he couldn't walk, the water on the floor like some kind of sewer making it impossible to maintain stealth, so he crept along the side of the slimy wall behind Mr. Chamberlain, who kept a steady pace for what seemed like twenty minutes. And finally, at the end of it was another set of stairs. Chamberlain climbed them and pushed open a metal door that was over his head, a lot more carelessly then he did the first time. Like he knew no one would be there.

Miles had no idea where they had come out, or why, but the door seemed to be in the middle of a field. He followed Mr. Chamberlain across the grass until finally a huge house, a mansion with castle pillars, came into view. Miles turned around to see where they had come from—to see if there were any landmarks, anything he recognized— and then he saw it, smack-dab in front of the house. The stone block. Fenced in, barbed-wired and impenetrable. On the fence was a sign: DEPARTMENT OF CORRECTIONS.

*The prison?*

Miles ducked behind a bush as Mr. Chamberlain walked up to the door, huge and wooden. He rang the bell. It opened, and Mr. Chamberlain entered. Miles made his move up to one of the slightly cracked windows.

Inside the house was beautiful. Full of old things. Sophisticated tile floors. Curtains the color of milk, made of some kind of fine fabric—linen or silk. Big furniture that looked like it had been carved in ancient villages by ancient people. An extravagant chandelier. A cat-o'-nine-tails hung on the wall in between a set of portraits encased in frames as ornate as the fancy clothes of the painted subjects.

Miles felt like he had been there before. Tried to shake the déjà vu, but couldn't. Where had he seen this place? He spotted an old cabinet across the room complete with shelves stocking crystal trinkets.

*Wait . . . no. There's no way. It . . . can't be.* It finally hit him. He had been pushed into that trinket cabinet before, remembered the glass breaking, slicing into his back. He could still feel the sting from the shattered shards, even though it had only happened in his dreams. His night-mares. The one where he was fighting Uncle Aaron. This was the house. *This was the house!*

Miles listened as closely as he could as men of all ages gathered around one really, really old man with a pasty face and a long white beard. It was the man Uncle Aaron and Mr. Chamberlain turned into in the nightmares. He stood in the middle of the stairwell addressing his guests, like the fanciest, stiffest dinner party of all time.

The old man began to speak, and Miles adjusted his

ears to hear clearly through the sliver of space between window and sill.

"Good evening, Chamberlains."

"Good evening, Warden," they all said in unison like zombies. Real zombies.

*Warden?* Miles couldn't believe what he was hearing.

"Is there any news to report? Any prospects?" the Warden asked.

Hands went up from the crowd.

A short, skinny man with red moppy hair and freckles raised his hand.

"Yes, Mr. Chamberlain?"

*Yes, Mr. Chamberlain.* Miles heard that phrase over and over again as the men in the room announced their weekly victories. *Dante Jones has dropped out, thanks to the pressure.* And *I've convinced my principal that I feel threatened by Marcus Williams. He's loud and has no place, no right to be there.* And *I'm working on shifting bus routes to make sure they can't get there. That'll take care of a lot without us even trying.* And *Just found out Randolph Duncan is in foster care. He's nothing. He has no one.*

"Let's make sure *he* gets snatched, this week," the Warden instructed. "He's already invisible, which makes it easier."

And on and on. Miles listened, trying not to be sick or burst through the window and smash the place, which, he knew, would be a terrible idea. A few minutes later Mr. Chamberlain spoke up. *His* Mr. Chamberlain.

"Ah, before we hear your testimony, Mr. Chamberlain, first let me compliment you on this evening's attire. You remind of my old friend, the great Jefferson Davis here." The Warden pointed to one of the old portraits on the wall.

"Thank you, Warden. It's an honor. I'd like to report that I've been watching the young man Miles Morales."

"Yes, yes, Miles Morales." Miles's eyes widened as he heard his name. "The *Super Hero*." Sarcasm dripped from the Warden's voice. *Super Hero? But . . . how could they know?* The mere thought of anyone, especially Mr. Chamberlain, and all the others in that room, being made aware of Miles's secret caused his stomach to flip. The entire room rumbled in amusement as the Warden continued. "Extraordinary power is made only for extraordinary people. And, hear me, you have to be born extraordinary, with pure blood and a strong mind. It's not his fault he's a descendant of filth, but it's dangerous to everyone that he thinks he can be more than that. Yes, Mr. Chamberlain, I've been watching him too. I've journeyed through his thoughts. I've whispered to him in his sleep, the same way I've done most of the men in his family. And though he's a bit more resistant, we have to correct him. And to do that, we must break him."

"Yes, sir. I tried framing him for stealing . . . sausages. Though he wiggled out of expulsion, he still lost his job, putting his parents in more of a bind." Another low laugh spread around the room. "In short, I think we're close to breaking him."

Miles's face crumpled. Reflexively, he balled his hands into fists.

"Ah. That's fantastic. Do you have anyone else you're watching?" the Warden asked.

"Not actively, but there is a boy named Judge."

"Judge?" the Warden scoffed. "The *irony*. Well, Mr. Chamberlain, keep us posted, and well done."

"Thank you, Warden." Mr. Chamberlain stepped back into the crowd.

The Warden lifted a glass to his lips and drank. "I remember a few hundred years ago, back when America really worked. When labor was not something that had to be bargained for, but something that was readily available by beings that would have no purpose unless we gave them the purpose of servitude. That's what we need to return to. That's our mission." The Warden paused, took a sip of the glass. His swallow looked like a small animal scurrying down his throat. He wiped his mouth. "It disgusts me, what I see now. So we have work to do. More good, important work. Correcting. Remember our motto: *Distract and defeat.*"

The Warden lifted his glass and made a toast.

"To the Chamberlains."

"To the Chamberlains!" And the cocktail party started.

Miles backed away from the window. He was still in camo mode, but with that many people watching, it always felt like someone could see him. He dashed back across the field toward the prison until he reached the metal door in the ground. He yanked it, but it didn't budge. Miles tightened his grip and yanked it harder, ripping it off the hinges. Luckily, there were no prison guards monitoring the back field. Then again, if anybody actually did break out of the prison, made it over the stone wall, and somehow got through the barbed wire fence, they'd have nowhere to run but straight to the Warden's house, where, clearly, trouble was awaiting.

Miles jumped back into the tunnel and sprinted through the sewer until he finally came back to steps underneath the auditorium. He put his ear to the door to make sure no one was there making out. Once he knew it was clear, he kicked the locked door open, ran back down the side of the building, and slipped back into the winding-down party, where he found Ganke still standing in the middle of the floor, ramrod straight, his hands pressed together like a monk in prayer.

## CHAPTER ELEVEN

"**M**iles, you're being weird," Ganke said as they walked from the auditorium back to their dorm. "We just came from the best party ever, and you're acting like it was just another Saturday night at the Morales house. Better yet, you're acting like it was last night at the Lee house."

"I'll tell you what happened when we get back to the room. I can't talk about it out here," Miles said through his teeth.

"Well, can I at least just tell you about the prank? So, all night, they were bringing out those bowls of punch, right? So on one of the refill rounds, there was a girl waiting to get some and she dipped the scoop in, and when she brought it up, she screamed. Dude, I mean she really wailed. It was crazy. And guess why?" Miles didn't respond. "Because she thought there were fingers in it! But they *weren't* fingers, they were sausages! The seniors are geniuses!" Ganke hooted, but then awkwardly pinched his laughter off after noticing the look on Miles's face. Miles wasn't amused. How could he be when he had just found out Mr. Chamberlain stole those sausages as part of a plan to sabotage him? *Maybe the seniors were geniuses,* Miles thought . . . *in conjunction with the history department.* Or maybe not. "Know what? Never mind. You had to be there," Ganke said.

Kids were everywhere, many of their costumes now a mess of streaky makeup. They were screaming and playing around, the sugar in the candy kicking them into overdrive. Miles moved quickly through them, though he glanced at all of the faces to make sure he wasn't overlooking Alicia. But she was nowhere to be found. And that was probably for the best. Miles wasn't in any shape to talk to her about . . . anything.

But once they reached their room, Miles tried to explain it all to Ganke.

"So you followed him?" Ganke asked, peeling the pink swim cap from his head.

"Yeah, man. I followed him to a door on the side of the auditor—"

"Wait." Ganke tapped his shoulders as if calling time-out. "So . . . you missed the whole party? I just thought maybe you missed the end. Snuck out with Alicia or something."

"I was there. But then I left, because when I was talking, or . . . trying to talk to her, Chamberlain came over and messed with me, and my spidey-sense started going off, and I've been saying something is up with him. That he's not—"

"*Wait*. Time-out. Time. OUT!" Ganke put his hands up, again. "So you *did* talk to Alicia? And how was that?" Ganke bounced his heavy eyebrows.

"Ganke. I don't know because I had to leave."

"What? Why?"

"That's what I'm trying to tell you!" Miles said, pounding his own legs. "Listen. I followed Chamberlain. He went to this other door on the side of the auditorium. He had a key for it. It led down into like a sewer or something, and after a whole lot of walking we came out on the other end, which was at the prison."

Miles explained everything, the words coming out faster than his brain was working. He told Ganke about how the house matched the house in his dreams, about the Warden, about how they were targeting certain students, and were especially targeting Miles.

"They know I'm Spider-Man," he said.

Ganke sat quietly.

Miles set the zombie mask he was wearing on the bed and yanked open his closet door. He kicked a few shoe boxes out of the way, and got into the corner, where he yanked out his Spider-Man suit.

"What are you doing, Miles?" Ganke asked, concerned.

Miles laid the suit out on the bed. "You know what I'm doing."

"Tonight?" Ganke stood up from the bed as if he was ready to try to physically stop Miles. "You want to go fight a whole house full of people? Think, Miles." Ganke tapped his finger to his temple. "From what it sounds like, Mr. Chamberlain and all the other Mr. Chamberlains are being controlled by this old dude. He's obviously the guy you need to be after."

Miles sighed, then sat on his bed next to the black-and-red suit. He stared at it. "You're right. I'm just so . . . so . . ."

"I know. But man, you got that break-a-desk look on your face again. And the last time that happened you, well, you broke a desk."

"Shut up, man." Miles allowed himself to calm down.

"I'm just saying, sleep on it." Ganke sat back on his bed, kicked his shoes off, and yawned. "Just promise me that if you, in fact, do sleep on it, you won't be crawling on the ceiling and all that. It's Halloween night and I just don't think I can take it."

Miles threw Ganke's rubber mask at him.


Miles lay flat on his back, his hands cupping the back of his head. He stared at the ceiling and let all the tangled thoughts from the week wash over him. His neighborhood, the only place he'd ever known as home, was full of all the complicated things that made him who he was. His neighbors like Ms. Shine, watering her flowers, and Fat Tony, counting and recounting his money. Frenchie, walking her son to the basketball court. Neek, who had been "snatched," and how he used to peek through the curtains afraid that one day there might be a tank rolling down the block. House and the barbershop boys, rooting for Miles, seeing him as one of the golden representatives of the neighborhood. Miles's mother and father, trying their best to provide a good life, with better opportunities than they had.

Miles thought about Uncle Aaron, the good in him, the bad in him, the secret life they lived together, and the secret death they shared. He thought about Austin, how he was unconsciously following in his father's footsteps down a path he didn't even know was paved for him the moment he was born. He thought about the dreams that the Warden had planted. The nightmares he and Austin shared. The white cats. The reminders that they had bad blood. Were bad. Were meant to do bad. Be bad. That everyone was after them.

Miles thought about his father's three friends, Sip, Carlo, and John John, slapping cards on the table and talking trash to each other about the good ol' days. And how there was always a Mr. Chamberlain, an adult working at a school, leaning on them, working them raw. And then, after thinking about all these things, Miles thought of Alicia. Alicia the beautiful Halloween humpback, who he'd given a sijo—his salsa—to. And before Miles could even think about whether or not she'd liked it, if she'd smiled, he was asleep.

## CHAPTER TWELVE

Miles slept on it. Barely. Though he practically passed out from exhaustion, it was a stunted sleep, as he kept waking up over and over again, his heart pounding, his head spinning, nausea overcoming him. There was no way he could get a good night's rest knowing what he knew. After seeing what he'd seen. So on the fourth wake-up, as the sun finally started to warm the sky with its orange, Miles decided to get up. He slipped out of bed and out of the room. The hallway was littered with candy wrappers and random pieces of costumes that most likely became pretend weapons for teenage boys hopped-up on sugar and ego. Once Miles made it to the bathroom, empty but still damp, he climbed into one of the shower stalls and turned it on, the cold water sending a shock through his body before warming quickly to hot. The steam engulfed him as he stood there, turning the knob hotter and hotter to see just how much pain he could take.

After the shower, he went to the sink to brush his teeth. He squeezed the toothpaste onto the toothbrush, then slipped it into his mouth and glanced up. He was Aaron. He closed his eyes, opened them. Austin. He staggered back, wagging his head, white foam dripping from his mouth. He glanced back at the mirror and saw himself. Spat in the sink. Ran the cold water from the faucet, making a bowl with his hands and splashing his face, cleaning the toothpaste from it, and trying to snap himself out of whatever delusional breakdown was happening. He toweled his face from the nose down, patting it while staring into his own eyes in the mirror. He dried his mouth and his chin, then pulled the towel away, his skin no longer his own. The brown of it now alabaster and thin. Its smoothness replaced by long, stringy hair.

"*Wha?*" Miles panicked, his heart dropping to his stomach. He pinched his eyes shut one more time, keeping them closed as he chanted to himself, "Wake up, Miles. Wake up." Then he slowly put his hand up to his chin, to feel . . . nothing. Just skin, again. The beard was gone.

Ganke was still asleep when Miles got back in the room. He dressed quickly—jeans and a sweatshirt—then slipped out of the room again and headed downstairs. It was Sunday morning. A familiar time of day—usually when Miles would be walking to church with his mother.

"Father Jamie's got a word for us, Miles," his mother would say, the sound of her high heels clacking up the sidewalk. But Miles was never that enthused about it. However, this Sunday, Miles was yearning to sit next to his mother in the pew while she passed him candy. The two of them sharing a hymnal, singing off-key. So he headed to where he'd never gone the entire time he'd been at Brooklyn Visions Academy—to the campus chapel.

The weather wasn't nearly as beautiful as it had been earlier in the week, but it was definitely just as peaceful. The sunlight of daybreak was now being overshadowed by the gloom of clouds. A light rain fell, which usually would've been a turnoff, but on this particular morning was refreshing.

The chapel was located on the other side of campus, so Miles meandered down the littered cobblestone pathways between palatial buildings, all marble and brick. He walked past the store, figured Winnie was probably there. Thought about stopping in, but decided to keep moving. He passed the library, EX NIHILO NIHIL FIT engraved in the white stone above the gigantic double doors. Mrs. Tripley was probably in there, asleep. An image of her dressed like Mary Shelley—which was basically her dressed in a black ball gown—curled up between the stacks popped in Miles's head. It made him smile.

He continued on, and eventually got to the quad, where the raindrops pimpled and dimpled the fountain water. Miles flashed back to the open mic. Instantly, the drizzle felt colder, his sweatshirt, slowly wetting, now heavier than it was a few steps before. So he moved on, and just beyond the quad was the chapel.

It was a small white building, two steps, nothing fancy or ornate. Nowhere near as regal as the rest of the campus. The doors were closed, but Miles figured the church was always open. Maybe he could go to confession, get some things off his chest, apologize for what he wanted to do to the Warden—what he was planning to do. His mother would be proud of him if she knew he'd gone. But when Miles climbed the steps and got to the door, yanked the tarnished brass handle, the door didn't budge. Miles yanked again. It was locked. So he sat down on the steps and waited.

It wasn't long before people started showing up. But they weren't other students looking for a quiet place to pray. Instead they were men dressed in green jumpsuits and dirty boots, carrying trash bags and poles with a spike on the end. The maintenance workers were cleaning up the mess made the night before—the candy wrappers and soda cans and candy wrappers and more candy wrappers.

Miles watched as they punched the spike through small bits of paper, then shook them into the bags. It reminded him of what his father had made him do a week before, cleaning up the trash on his block. The only difference was that these guys were getting paid for it. Still, Miles couldn't help but think about his dad telling him that he was responsible for his block, and that being a hero wasn't always just the big things, but also the small things, like picking up trash. Miles stood up and walked over to one of the guys.

"Morning." Miles spoke to a guy who had a hood

yanked over his head and earbuds in his ears. The guy snatched an earbud out.

"What you say?"

"I said, good morning," Miles repeated.

The guy nodded. "Morning." Then he started to put the bud back in his ear when Miles stopped him.

"Sorry, but can I ask you something?" Miles started. The guy nodded again. "You think I can maybe help out?"

"Help out?" The guy snorted. "Yo, little man wanna help out," he said, turning to the guys around him.

"Help out?" a different guy wearing an orange hat said. He had a toothpick sticking out from the side of his mouth. "Um . . . you do know we cleaning this crap up, right?"

"Yeah, I know."

They all looked around at each other. Shrugged. Then Earbuds gave Miles his spiked pole. "I'll hold the bag," he said, obviously happy to be passing off some of the work. "We already did one walk-through, and now we walking through again, heading back toward the dorms."

"Cool."

As they moved from one part of campus to the next, the maintenance crew made small talk with Miles, but mainly Miles just listened as they conversed with each other about their weekends.

"Yo, any of y'all ever had the catfish at Peaches?" Orange Hat asked.

"Peaches?" This from a guy with a beard, low but thick like black felt.

"Yeah, Peaches. You know, the spot Benji used to wait

tables at. Over there off Macdonough," Orange Hat explained. Miles's ears perked when he heard the name. *Benji, Benji. Where have I . . . ?* He wiped rain from his forehead and pushed the stake through the heart of a fun-size Snickers wrapper.

"Where Benji at, anyway? Ain't he supposed to be here?" Toothpick asked, shaking his head.

"Ain't nobody seen him since Monday, when he came to work all lumped up. After that, no call, no show," Black Felt said. Miles glanced up, then immediately darted his eyes back down at the ground searching for the next piece of litter. *Benji. Not . . . not the one from the basketball court. Can't be,* Miles thought.

"He probably off trying out for the Knicks, again." This was from a guy named Ricky, a short dude with tall-dude pants on, bunched and gathered around the tops of his boots.

"He ain't never tried out for the Knicks," Earbud said.

"He told me he did," Ricky said.

"He also told you he had proof he had the highest vertical on earth." Everyone burst into laughter. Everyone but Miles.

"He probably just quit this crappy job," Earbud said, opening the trash bag so Miles could shake off the spike. The drizzle finally started to let up.

"Without telling us?" Toothpick asked. "I called him and everything. Twice."

"And he ain't hit you back?" Black Felt asked.

"Nah. And that was days ago. It's like he just disappeared."

"What you mean, *disappeared*?" Now Miles butted in. He didn't mean to, but he just couldn't help it. The four green-suited men shot glances at him.

"You know Benji?" Ricky asked, his tone slightly harder than it was seconds before. His voice made it clear he was half asking sincerely, and half telling Miles to mind his own business.

"Um . . . nah. I just . . ."

And before Miles could try to hack up the rest of the words lodged in his throat, Orange Hat jumped back in. "Yo, whatever. The point is, if y'all ain't never had the catfish from that spot, Peaches, do yourself a favor. They got the cornmeal batter and all that. Mad good." He reached over and grabbed the trash-stabber from Miles, signaling that the job was done. They were back in front of the dorms. "You too, shorty," Orange Hat said to Miles. "I'm sure it's probably better than what y'all eating at this bland-ass school."

## CHAPTER THIRTEEN

"Good morning, uh . . . I was gonna say *sunshine*, but you're soaking wet, so . . . good morning, rainstorm," Ganke said as Miles came back in the room. Ganke was sitting in his desk chair scooping cereal from a bowl, watching TV.

Miles didn't respond. Just sat on his bed and cradled his face in his hands. Benji didn't deserve to be snatched. And even though Miles wasn't sure if it had actually happened to Benji, he had a feeling, one deep in the pit of his stomach, that that was the case.

"You good?" Ganke asked, spinning his chair toward Miles. Miles continued to hide his face.

"Yeah," he said, his voice muffled by his hands. "Went down to the chapel." Miles lifted his face.

"The campus chapel?" Ganke sounded surprised.

"What, your mother came to you in your dreams and told you to get your butt up for church?" Miles didn't laugh.

"It wasn't open. Too early, I guess. But I still got a message." Suddenly, Miles got up from the bed, squatted, and reached underneath the twin frame. He swiped a few times, before finally knocking forward his web-shooters. He set them on the bed, then dug back into the closet and pulled out his suit again. "And now I have to deliver one."

"Miles, what are you doing?" Ganke asked. Miles continued to get dressed. "Miles." Ganke set his bowl on his desk. "It's not even eight in the morning."

"Look, I slept on it. Just like you told me." Miles peeled off his wet clothes, dried himself off with his towel, then stretched the suit over his body like a second skin. "And now I have to go."

He grabbed his mask, walked over to the mirror.

Ganke stood up.

Miles slowly rolled the mask down over his forehead, then over his eyes. Like always, he closed them for a split second, just until the holes lined up. Then he opened them and continued stretching the mask over his nose, mouth, and chin. He looked at himself in the mirror again. Spider-Man.

"And I think what you said last night was right. You kill the head, the feet die too. That old man is the head. And I have stop him. He's hurting so many people. People we know. People we don't know. People who aren't even alive yet, man. He's hurting my family, people in my neighborhood, me . . . I just, I won't be able to do anything until I do this. What good is it being a hero if I can't even save myself?"

"And you're sure about all this?" Ganke asked. He looked at Miles without an ounce of joke on his face, no snark in his voice. Just Ganke, the closest person Miles had to a brother. Someone who loved him.

"I'm sure." Miles nodded. "I'm not guessing. I know these things. And knowledge is power."

"And with great power . . ."

"Comes great responsibility," Miles finished, holding his hand up for Ganke. Ganke slapped his palm in Miles's, gripped it tight—eye to eye—before Miles turned to the window, shoved it open, camouflaged himself into red brick against blue sky, and climbed out.

Miles crawled along the side of the building before jumping to the ground and running across the campus to the auditorium. Once he got back to the same door he'd followed Mr. Chamberlain into the night before, he bent the steel back just enough to slip inside. Miles came out of camouflage and leaped from the steps down into the tunnel, where the light was swallowed by the tunnel's darkness, water splashing him. He sprinted through the tunnel like an express train. His brain wouldn't quit racing—his family name, the suspension, his uncle, his father, his neighborhood, Austin, everyone who came before him, everyone coming after him.

*Everyone coming after him.*

After a few minutes of flashing through the tunnel,

Miles reached the overhead double doors. He listened. He could hear the crickets jumping through the field, an airplane in the sky still miles from passing overhead. But not the sound of grass blades bending, which meant no feet. He pushed the gate open, climbed out, and looked behind him. The fence, higher than most buildings, blocked off the back stone wall of the prison.

He ran toward the house, slipped right back to the window he had peered through the night before. He hunkered down like a soldier waiting on the order to attack. The Warden was there, dressed in trousers and a white dress shirt, sitting in a huge chair, sipping from a mug. The sun shone through the window, filtered through the crystal trinkets in the cabinet against the wall, creating a kaleidoscope of rainbows, which would've been a beautiful image under different circumstances. An image meant for an art gallery or a museum.

A white cat came from behind the couch, the color of fresh snow. It leaped onto the couch, cozied up on the leg of the old man, who stroked its fur gently. Miles could hear the cat's purring, a soft, satisfied rumble, as the cat licked around its own mouth, stretching it into a fang-brandishing yawn. Again, Miles looked on, mesmerized by how sweet it all seemed. A rich man enjoying Sunday morning with his pet cat. Miles had always wanted a pet. Not a cat, though. He preferred dogs, but his father always said having a dog was like having another child, another mouth to feed. *And who's gonna walk it? And what if it bites you, Miles?* his father would say. And whenever

Miles would try to argue that it wouldn't bite, his father would say, *If it got teeth, it'll bite.*

And that sweet-looking cat had teeth. And so did that seemingly helpless old man, whose weathered body looked like it was papier-mâché. He had teeth too. Teeth that apparently had fallen into the mug he was sipping from, because he stuck his finger in and dug one out as if it were a chip of ice. Miles watched as the Warden positioned it back into whatever slot it had slipped from and pressed it with his thumb to his top row, seemingly forcing this disgusting chomper back into his gum line.

*Gross.* Miles shuddered. And just then the Warden glanced over at the window. Miles was still camouflaged but felt the need to drop below the windowsill anyway. He immediately felt silly, and stood up, knowing that he looked like grass, sky, stone, and gate. The Warden set his cup down on a side table, rose to his feet, the cat jumping from his lap to the floor. He walked over to the window, stood in front of it, gazing out into the field, ogling the prison, the big cement block, the construction on the side of it for expansion. He looked at it as if it were a shiny car, or a child he was proud of—his baby. Miles stood right in front of him, inhaling the age from the Warden's skin through the glass. It smelled like sweat and soil. But Miles wasn't concerned, and instead turned his attention to the cat, who he knew could see him. *Take it easy, kitty. Take it easy.* The cat looked at Miles, its tail waving back and forth the same way he'd seen a few days before when a similar cat, if not the same cat, was on Neek's stoop. Suddenly, the cat, who had been glaring at Miles, went into attack mode—back arched, hair spiked, hissing. *Calm down, kitty,* Miles said to himself, putting a finger to his mouth in a shushing gesture. The Warden took a step back, drawing Miles's eyes to him. His face hardened into viciousness.

*Wait. No way . . . He can't. . . .*

But he could. Somehow, he too could see Miles.

The Warden took off running, the cat dashing back behind the couch. Miles took a few steps back, then, like a human missile, torpedoed through the window. The glass exploded into the room, jagged shards everywhere, as Miles went from human missile straight into a forward roll, up onto his feet, and into an attack stride. He reached the Warden before the Warden reached the cat-o'-nine-tails hanging on the wall. Miles grabbed him by the shoulder—a shoulder that felt like a doorknob beneath fabric—whipping the ancient man around.

The Warden, in a fit of panic, took a wild swing, aiming for Miles's face. Miles backed away, avoiding the punch, but it still created some space between them. Then the Warden squared up, lifted his hands, old-school-style, wheeling his fists around almost as if he was doing some kind of dance. A salsa.

"You fool. You didn't think I could see you, did you?" he said, still winding up. "But when you've lived centuries, you have a different kind of vision. You can see all the things that don't seem to be really there." His lip curled up into a snarl, his teeth broken off like wood. "Like *opportunity.*" Then he came charging at Miles, his fists flying much faster and much harder than Miles expected.

Left, left, duck. Then the Warden surprised Miles by throwing a right uppercut to his chin. He bit down on his tongue. Heard his teeth cut the flesh. Blood filled his mouth, along with a searing sting. Before Miles could recover, the Warden threw two more punches, stiff jabs to Miles's nose. Miles's ears rang, and his eyes watered as he was totally caught off guard by the Warden's speed and strength. *Isn't this man hundreds of years old? Why is he not falling apart?* But there was no time to think about any of these things because the Warden cocked his leg up and planted a foot in Miles's chest, knocking him back against the massive front door. Then the old man came rushing. He threw a flurry of punches, combinations that most boxers couldn't throw. Miles did his best to block as many as he could before finally, in a state of desperation, he grabbed a lamp off the side table next to him—the shade, red, green, and purple stained glass—and cracked it over the Warden's head. The glass shattered, bright-colored shards falling like sprinkles on a sundae. Exactly like in Miles's nightmare.

Almost exactly.

The Warden hit the floor, and Miles shot some web to trap him there, but only a small amount came sputtering from the shooter. *Oh no. Don't tell me. . . .* The Warden, smirking again, rolled backward and back up onto his feet. Blood dripped from his ashen face, but it wasn't red. It was blue. And thick. It ran down his white shirt and across the mosaic tile floor.

Miles tried to shoot web again. But nothing.

"Oh, what a splendid sight," the Warden teased, dabbing the blood from his face with a finger. "What becomes of the spider that's lost its web? Does it still have the right to bear the name of spider?" Then, before Miles could attack, the Warden stretched his arms out like wings and grabbed the edges of the room. It was as if everything—the room, the floor, the couches, the paintings, the blood and glass, even Miles himself—was all just some kind of strange projection being shown on a huge piece of fabric. Like it wasn't real. Like it could be grabbed, folded. And that's exactly what the Warden did. Gripped the edges of the room, the seams of whatever Miles could see, and pulled them closer, like drawing curtains, folding in—folding up—reality. He closed the world in, more and more, tighter and tighter, until finally clapping the entire room in on Miles. Everything went dark for a split second, and when Miles could see again, the Warden opening his hands wide, Miles had absolutely no idea where he was. Or who he was. He patted his chest; the webbing on the suit was unfamiliar. Miles couldn't think of his name. Or where he was from. Or what he was doing in a bodysuit in the middle of nowhere. It was as if he'd been erased. As if there was no Rio and Jefferson, no Aaron, no Ganke. No Spider-Man. *Tabula rasa.*

While Miles staggered around the room, hazy, the Warden took full advantage and whaled on him. Miles couldn't see him but felt every strike. To the kidneys and ribs, to the sternum, and to the jaw. Miles was getting pummeled, and swung his arms at nothing, trying his best to connect his fists to something that wasn't physically there.

Fortunately, the trance only lasted about fifteen seconds before Miles blinked back to himself. Before the white space that had become his reality unfolded, like a fan being spread open revealing a beautiful image, rich with color and life. Except this image wasn't so beautiful for Miles. He was back to where he'd never left—the Warden's house, with full memory of who he was and what he was doing there. It was like how he thought about the security camera. That there would be a time jump but nobody would notice. Except in this case, he was stuck in the blank gap and he was the nobody who wouldn't notice.

What he did notice was the Warden, who had just grabbed his cat-o'-nine-tails from the wall.

"Your life is a nightmare!" the Warden howled, holding the tasseled whip. "And there's nothing you can do about it." Instead of trying to hit Miles with the flogger, the Warden cocked it back and heaved the entire thing at Miles. The easiest and most obvious thing for Miles to do would be to simply step out of the way. A simple dodge. But before he could, the handle of the cat-o'-nine-tails became the body of an actual nine-tailed cat in midair. Not the small cats Miles had been seeing around, like the one hiding somewhere behind the Warden's couch. But a huge beast, twice the size of a bear, gnashing at him. It arched its back, its hair raising into sharp spikes, so tall that if the ceilings weren't so high in the Warden's mansion the spikes would've left holes. Miles faced off with the animal, moving slowly as the cat watched him, waiting for the moment to pounce on him and tear him to shreds. Its nine tails snaked around the room, the hair on them like razors and the ends hardened and whittled to sharp points. The tails rose up behind the catlike dragon and jutted forward violently every few seconds.

"Here, kitty," Miles taunted, craning his neck to make sure he could still see the Warden. His eyes on the cat, those teeth, those tails. Then, his eyes on the Warden, who had now dashed across the room over to the painting of Jefferson Davis. The cat hissed, made a swipe, but not a full swipe. Instead it was more of a test to get a feel for its prey. Miles reflexively rubbered his body, bending backward as if he had no bones, the claw just grazing his torso, taking strips of his suit with it. *Watch the Warden,* he said to himself, sidestepping into the corner. He touched where the suit had been ripped. Felt his flesh, checked for blood. Only a little. The claws barely broke the skin. *Watch the Warden.* Miles, with one eye still on the giant cat, watched as the Warden pushed the huge painting to the side, revealing a hidden lever on the wall. He yanked it down, sounding a buzzing alarm. The buzz was the same as the one in the prison. The one that sounded like an electrocution. The one used when guards were being called. Miles swallowed hard, knowing that that couldn't have been a good sound or a good sign, but he also knew that whatever it meant wasn't going to stop the problem he had right in front of him. "Here, kitty, kitty, kitty," Miles called again to the cat.

Miles's first instinct was to slip back into camo, but then he remembered that it wouldn't matter. The cat would still be able to see him. Not to mention, the Warden could, too. Miles realized that his only hope would be to take advantage of the tails.

So Miles jumped at the cat, bucking to get it to snap at him. And it did. It took a hard swipe, and Miles quickly sprang onto the wall, avoiding the cat's attack, which left huge gashes in the clay. Miles skittered around, jumping from corner to corner, the cat swinging at Miles like he was a dangling chew toy, but missing, leaving destructive tiger stripes on the walls in its wake. Finally, the now-frustrated cat used one of its tails to strike, but Miles dodged that as well, and it drilled straight into the wall. The razors locked into the stone and clay. The cat struck with another tail, missing again. Another tail caught. And on and on. Miles bolted around the room, calling out for the cat, whose razor tails flung here and there, jamming into walls, and even into the ceiling, hooking into the grout. Moments later, the cat was trapped, all nine tails spread around the room, locking the body of the giant feline in place. And just like that, the monstrous animal let out a piercing shriek and became a simple whip again.

"You can't beat me!" Miles called out to the Warden, who ran for the whip. Miles bounded from the wall, drop-kicking the Warden in the chest—returning the favor from before—knocking him back against the Davis painting; the huge frame smacked loose from the wall, crashing down on the Warden. The frame landed on his neck, and the painting fell over him, the canvas stretching and bowing over the old man's head. By the time he pushed it off of him, Miles had already grabbed the nine-tailed whip.

"You don't know what to do with that. You don't have it in you," the Warden snarled, flashing a gap in his teeth. He slipped his tongue in the space, then spat blue slime on the floor. "You don't even know who you are." Miles started swinging the whip slowly so as not to accidentally hit himself. He zeroed in on the Warden. "You don't even know who I am!" And like changing the stations on a television, the Warden's face switched. First to Miles's father's. *Switch.* Austin's. *Switch.* Jefferson Davis's. *Switch.* Uncle Aaron's. "You're just like me!" *Switch.* Back to the Warden. "An insect! Something to be crushed under a thumb." The Warden let out a cackle, and again, reached out his arms, gripping the room, peeling it from the world like a sticker. This time, Miles turned to one of the huge windows. His heart jumping, his mind reeling, trying to convince himself that all this was real. That this wasn't a dream, a nightmare where you wake up still in a nightmare. *Wake up. No, you're awake. You're awake.* Out in the field he could see Chamberlains running toward the house. An army, ready for attack. Miles adjusted his eyes, pulling his attention away from the horde of evil coming toward him, and focused on his own reflection. He knew the Warden was folding the world up again, and it was best this time to brace himself for it. So he stared at the faded image of himself in the glass, rays of sun cutting through the top half of the reflection of the black-and-red mask.

And then . . . *CLAP!*

Darkness. And then whiteness. Blank. It was as if Miles had been sucked into a vacuum. An echo chamber. A humming in Miles's ear, a piercing sound ringing louder and louder until it abruptly stopped.

Silence.

*Can you hear me? Hello? Can you hear me? Can you hear us? Listen to us. Listen closely. Our names are Aaron, Austin, Benny, Neek, Cyrus, John, Carlo, Sherman. Benji. Our names are Rio, Frenchie, Winnie, Alicia. Our name is Miles Morales. We are sixteen. We are from Brooklyn. We are Spider-Man.*

Darkness.

*This is all in our minds.*

Darkness.

*This is all in your mind.*

*This is all in your mind. . . .*

And then, light. It had only been a split second. A blink. And Miles was still in the house. Still holding the cat-o'-nine-tails. Still looking at the window, his reflection in the glass. Nothing changed.

"What?" The Warden staggered back, shaking his head at the failed attempt at another mind warp. Miles smiled. But his smile was cut short by the Chamberlains surrounding the house, trying to force themselves through the broken window, climbing up onto the porch, slamming into the door like the undead.

Miles knew he wouldn't be able to beat them all, so he turned back to the Warden and started toward him, the cat-o'-nine-tails clutched tight by his side, the tassels dangling, barbed. Again, he started swinging it lightly.

"Don't do that," the Warden said, holding up his hand. Miles stepped forward, still swinging it. "You don't know what you're doing, boy. You don't know how to wield that kind of power!" the Warden shouted as Miles swung the whip, the tails circling round and round like propeller blades. As they cut through the air, the whir got louder and louder. Without stepping any further, Miles simply let it go. The momentum of the tails carried the whip across the room, and just like when the Warden had thrown it, in midair, the whip morphed into a cat.

Just then, the door slammed open and the Chamberlains came charging in like troops infiltrating a camp. There were a few who finally got through the shattered window. Miles assumed a fighting stance, ready to take on whichever Chamberlain jumped first.

"Help me!" the Warden called to them. But before they could even make a move, the gigantic cat speared the old man with one of its tails.

Every Chamberlain froze. The cat struck the Warden with another tail. And another. Tail after tail darting into the old man, pushing through his body, nailing him to the wall in the same spot his friend Jefferson Davis had been hanging for years.

There was no more sound. Not from the cat, or the Chamberlains, or Miles. Not from the old grandfather clock. As if the world had been muted. And then, loud like a gust of wind, the Warden exhaled his last breath.

Fur from the nine-tailed monster blew through the room like a blizzard, leaving nothing but a house cat. No whip. The Chamberlains snapped out of their stupor, and in a quick moment of reflex, Miles camouflaged himself. They all looked around at each other, puzzled, but didn't say a word. They just walked out of the house and headed across the field, leaving Miles standing in the doorway staring after them, the prison in the distance and a white cat—two white cats—affectionately rubbing up against his leg.

## CHAPTER FOURTEEN

Miles climbed back through the window of their dorm and fell into the room. Ganke yelped, then paused the Nintendo game he'd been playing and rushed over to Miles to help him up.

"Jesus, man. You look like you took a beating," Ganke said, hoisting him up.

"Yeah, well, not nearly as bad as the one I gave." Miles pushed the words through his winces and yanked the mask from his face. "It was weird. He could see me, man, even when I was camouflaged. He looked right at me. Said that when you're as old as he was, you can see the things that people don't think are there."

"Oh man, he really is the boss of Mr. Chamberlain. Our Mr. Chamberlain. Talking all that crazy stuff. Like, what does that even mean?"

"He looked me in the face and said, *opportunity*." Miles shook his head. "Like *I* was the opportunity."

"Well, I bet he didn't expect 'the opportunity' to beat the hell out of him." Ganke reached out his fist for a pound. But Miles waved it off, afraid his wrist was too sore. "You did beat him, right?"

Miles nodded. Ganke sat back in his chair, relieved. Also a little proud.

Miles told Ganke the rest of the story, what the Warden said, the mind warping, the giant cat monster with nine tails, the way the Warden tried to sic the Chamberlains on him like zombie attack dogs.

"But when it was over, they just walked away. It was like they had all awakened from a dream. Like they had been sleepwalking and suddenly decided to go home. It was wild." Miles shook his head slightly. "But what really threw me, and it's still messing with me, is that they didn't say anything. They didn't wonder why or how they ended up at this crashed-up house behind the prison. They just kinda snapped out of whatever trance the Warden had them in and walked off. So what if . . . what if the trance wasn't like a *full* trance? I mean, if they knew where they were, and they didn't seem surprised, then maybe it wasn't a total mind control thing, right? Maybe it was a little mind control, and a little . . . I don't know, willingness."

"Or maybe the spell's not all the way broken yet. It might just take awhile to wear off, and tomorrow they'll all wake up feeling like normal people, with no memory of all this," Ganke suggested.

"Hmm. Maybe." Miles pondered for a moment before tacking on, "It's just crazy, man."

"Yeah it is," Ganke agreed, grimacing at Miles's wounds. "Yo, by the way," he continued, now moving the chair out of the way—video game controller dangling from it—so he could get to his desk. "While you were out doing . . . all of that"—Ganke pointed at the wounds—"I was in here playing video games to keep my mind off the fact that you might get yourself killed. And I was enjoying myself, just breaking bricks and going down sewer pipes— Wow . . . We're, like, in sync, man! Anyway, I was doing my thing until I got a bang on the door. Scared me to death, man. I literally almost dove out the window, that, by the way, *you* left open."

"Who was it?" Miles pressed his face lightly, feeling for any sore spots.

"Alicia."

His hand dropped. Miles turned toward Ganke, his eyes suddenly lively. "She told me to give this to you," Ganke said, holding up a folded piece of paper.

Miles almost killed himself trying to get across the room, tripping over the controller cord. Everything painful, none of it mattering. He snatched the paper and unfolded it, the smell of sandalwood ghosting up into his nose.

**YES, IT'S SANDALWOOD. AND . . .**

You don't think I see you, hiding in the window looking
at me, looking at you, looking for some sense in poetry;
But don't you know, poetry isn't the prize, it's the prelude.

Miles played video games with Ganke for the rest of the day, something he hadn't done all week. And between the gaming binge, Miles reread the poem, sniffed the paper like a weirdo. And once he climbed into bed that night and fell asleep, he stayed there, and woke up the next day rested. No bad dreams. No sweats. No crawling the walls. No haunting relatives. Just sleep.

Ganke was already up. He was staring at the ceiling, his phone on his chest, as Miles rolled over.

"Yo," Miles called. "You aight?"

Ganke slowly rolled his head to the side, nodded slightly. "Just texted my parents."

"Yeah?" Miles wiped crust from the side of his mouth. Drool was always a great sign of a good night's rest.

"Yeah. At the same time. Group text."

*Uh-oh,* Miles thought. Knowing Ganke, it could have been a crazy, off-the-cuff joke, or a text explosion of the emotions Miles had been watching him hold in.

"Uh-oh," Miles decided to say out loud. "What did you say?"

Ganke smirked, rolled his head back and returned his eyes to the ceiling.

"I told them I loved them."

"That's all?" Miles asked.

"Yeah." Ganke nodded. "And they both texted back, *I love you, too.*" Ganke's eyes shone with water. He blinked, wiped the tears away before they fell.

Miles sat up, his body still stiff. He felt an itch on his thigh, reached down to scratch it, and realized it was

Alicia's letter stuck to his leg. Miles unfolded it for what was probably the twentieth time and held it up to his face. He knew Ganke needed a laugh. Ganke always knew how to take the sting out of everything. Now Miles was going to try to return the favor.

"And *I* love *you*, Alicia," Miles said, in a high-toned squeal. "So, so much." He started kissing the paper, *kiss, kiss, kiss,* before shouting, "I spilled the salsa! Ganke, I spilled it! I spilled the salsa! *Wepa!*"

Ganke cracked a smile, and for Miles, that was enough.

As Miles headed to Blaufuss's class, he saw Alicia standing in a crowd outside the room with Winnie, Dawn, and . . . Ganke. Ganke glanced up and saw him, that signature smile wiped across his face as usual. Ganke mischievously waved him over, and Miles tried his best to send some sort of telepathic middle finger to his best friend. As he approached the group, Miles tried to take deep breaths to calm himself down.

*Wassup?* he said to himself.

*No. Hi. Hey,* he tried, but didn't like it. He was quickly approaching.

*What's good? No. Too much. But she from Harlem. So . . . maybe.*

And then he was standing in front of them. In front of her.

"Hey," Miles muttered.

"Wassup, Miles." Winnie spoke first. Then headed into the classroom, along with Dawn.

"*Hello*, Miles," Ganke said. Eyebrow bounce. Pinched laughter. Noticing the look on Miles's face, Ganke stuck his thumb up and moonwalked away.

"What's good?" Alicia asked, her lips twisted.

"I . . . um . . . I got your letter. Your poem." His stomach rumbled like he'd swallowed a car engine.

"And I got yours," she replied. Her voice was warm, confident, though Miles thought he could hear a slight tremor in it. "It was sweet."

"So was yours. I mean, it was—"

"How did you know it was sandalwood?" She cut to the chase, smiling.

Before Miles could answer, Ms. Blaufuss poked her head out of the classroom. "The bell's about to ring. Y'all coming in?"

"Do we have a choice?" Alicia asked, snarky.

"You always have a choice." Ms. Blaufuss winked.

After Ms. Blaufuss's class, when Miles was heading down to the cafeteria for lunch, he saw Mr. Chamberlain in the hallway. Miles knew there was a good chance Mr. Chamberlain would be at school. Why wouldn't he be? But what Miles didn't know was if Chamberlain would be different now that the Warden was dead. Stop treating him unfairly. *You chop off the head to stop the feet.* Just made sense to Miles, especially since he had experienced the Warden's mind games firsthand. Miles figured the best way to gauge this was to first see if Chamberlain's presence would trigger his spidey-sense. He walked up behind

Mr. Chamberlain. Felt nothing. No buzz. So he decided to test him in a different way—by speaking.

"Um, excuse me, Mr. Chamberlain?" Miles said. He was even brave enough to tap Mr. Chamberlain on the shoulder. He turned around. His face no different than it usually was. Tight, weird-looking, not the most pleasant mug Miles had seen, that's for sure. Miles stepped back, braced himself.

"Yes, Miles?"

*Miles?* Mr. Chamberlain hadn't called Miles anything other than Morales all year. Miles looked in Chamberlain's eyes, searching for the discomfort he always felt. But it wasn't there. Just a strange-looking, mean-faced man waiting on Miles to say something. "Can I help you?"

"Oh . . . um . . . you know what, never mind. I'll just ask when we get to class."

"You sure?"

"Yeah. Yes. Yes, sir," Miles said, turning around and continuing toward the cafeteria, a rush of satisfaction coming over him.

He told Ganke about it at lunch.

"Nothing happened?"

"Nothing. Even his tone of voice was different," Miles explained.

"Well, that makes sense, because I just got out of his class and he definitely seemed . . . I don't know, less weird." Ganke dipped a fry in ketchup. "Thank God for Spider-Man, huh?" He chomped down on the fry. "Speaking of, let me ask you, does, uh, Spider-Man get the girl?"

"Stop talking like we're in a movie, Ganke. *The girl has a name.*" Miles let his smile shine, but turned his face toward his food so it wouldn't be so blinding. "And . . . I think so."

"You *think* so? Y'all been doing this weird thing for like a year! And after all that prep work I did this morning. Told her about how you were kissing the paper and all that."

"What? Ganke!"

"I'm joking, man. Chill out." Ganke grabbed another fry and dragged it through the ketchup. "What really happened was she came to me talking about how she couldn't get over the way Chamberlain had treated you and how she's decided to organize some kind of protest with some folks, but she knew you wouldn't be with it, so to make you feel better she also called her grandma to see if she can cause a stink on the . . . whatever board she's part of, blah-blah-blah."

"Wait, what? She told you all that?" Miles asked, stealing one of Ganke's fries. "Well ain't no need for all that now," he said, fry in mouth.

"Right. But let me finish. *Then,* she asked me if you got the letter. Like, she hit me with the *Ganke, I know how you are. Did you remember to give Miles the letter?* Checkin' for you, kid."

"And you said?" Miles asked, watching Ganke eat another fry, nibbling it bit by bit until it was gone. Ganke turned to Miles.

"Does it matter?"

And it didn't. It didn't matter when the bell rang, and Miles and Ganke left the cafeteria. It didn't matter when Miles met Alicia in the hallway, waiting for him to walk to Mr. Chamberlain's class. It didn't matter when she told him the plan, the same thing she told Ganke, about the protest—*It was the second thing I had to tell you at the party*—how she was going to get everyone to turn their desks around and face the wall, force Chamberlain to feel ignored. How she was going to tell her grandmother to try to get Mr. Chamberlain fired, or when Miles told her not to do any of it, that he already had it handled. None of it mattered, because it was Monday, a new day, a new week at Brooklyn Visions Academy. Miles Morales felt full of purpose and hope. Hope for his mother and father, his community. Hope for his cousin, Austin, who he figured today might be being treated a little better in jail. Hope that he'd someday be able to live with what happened with Uncle Aaron, and until then, he'd be able to think about him in the same way he thought about himself—as complicated. As human.

Hope. The spider had done it. Just like Mrs. Tripley said—connected the past and the future, on one hand creating a new strong web, and on the other, tearing an old web apart.

But as Miles and Alicia reached Mr. Chamberlain's class, every student was diverting their eyes, just as they had done the Friday before. Not because of Alicia. Because of Miles. Because his desk was still on the floor.

"Miles." Mr. Chamberlain turned from the chalkboard

where he was scribbling his daily quote. "What was it you had to ask me?"

Miles didn't respond. He couldn't. The magic of this new Monday seemed to vanish immediately. "Well, if you're not going to answer, at least take your seat." He pointed to the empty chair next to the broken desk. Miles let out a breath. At least Chamberlain didn't point at the floor. Miles sat in his chair, his desk on the floor in front of him like a small pedestal. Alicia, still looking skeptical, took her seat in front of Miles. He looked up at the board. Instead of a strange quote from a historic figure, it simply said, MIDTERM EXAM THIS FRIDAY. He started jotting down notes.

"Miles."

Miles looked up.

"What are you doing?" Chamberlain asked.

"What you mean?" Miles asked, confused.

And then it happened.

Chamberlain pointed to the floor.

"We discussed this. New week, but same rules, son," Mr. Chamberlain explained, and even though his voice wasn't as cold as it had been the week prior, he was still saying the same thing. That Miles should work on the floor. "We just don't damage things and act like we didn't. We have to live with that. *You* have to live with that."

Alicia whipped around in her desk as Miles's face went numb. He understood what Mr. Chamberlain was saying— what was happening. That despite the mind control of the Warden being lifted, Miles was still Miles Morales, black and Puerto Rican from the "other" part of Brooklyn. The part of Brooklyn that Brooklyn Visions Academy didn't have much vision for at all. Miles Morales, from a family of criminals. A neighborhood of nobodies, at least to the Mr. Chamberlains of the world.

Miles pushed the chair out from behind him and dropped to his knee. Alicia reached for his hand.

"Miles." She shook her head. "Don't."

He looked up at her, all eyes, all heart. "I won't." He grabbed his backpack, his notebook, and headed to the front of the class.

"What are you gonna do, leave?" Mr. Chamberlain asked, a tinge of sarcasm in his voice.

Miles stood in front of him. A slight smirk crept onto his face. "No." And at that moment, Miles walked over to Mr. Chamberlain's desk, big and wooden in the front corner of the class, covered in papers and books. Pens, felt tip and ballpoint. Pencils, no. 2 and mechanical. And of course, one can of sausage. Miles went behind it, pulled the chair from under it, and had a seat.

A thunder of laughter and disbelief rumbled through the class. Alicia smiled, wide.

"Miles. Get up," Mr. Chamberlain said, trying to keep his cool.

"Mr. Chamberlain, why would I sit on the floor, on my knees, in your class, a class that I need to do well in, a class that I need to be focused in, when this totally unoccupied desk is just sitting here?" Miles said, cheekily. He immediately thought about how Ganke would've loved this.

"You think this is funny, Miles? You think this is a joke?"

"No, sir. I don't. I really, really don't." Miles clenched his hands together on the desktop. "Now, I have a question for you." Miles looked Mr. Chamberlain in the eye. Mr. Chamberlain stood with his arms folded, scowling. "Do you think I'm an animal?"

"What? What are you talking about? Just get up from my desk, or I'll have you suspended!"

"Or maybe an insect? Some spider you think deserves to be crushed under your thumb?" At this Mr. Chamberlain paused, just a slight hesitation, a glimmer of something he knew but didn't know. Something he felt, but couldn't place. Miles nodded, and before Chamberlain could say anything else, before he could use the intercom system to contact campus police, Miles proclaimed, "I am a person." He looked at Alicia, now feeling a little embarrassed because his big finish was ruined by his inability to remember the rest of what she said that day in class.

Alicia side-eyed him, then, realizing what he was trying to say, she joined him. "We are people," she said.

"We are people," Miles repeated, his memory jogged. "Everybody, repeat after Alicia." He waved his arms as if he was welcoming the class into something. Into his trouble. And the class, still ready for the protest that Alicia had planned, fell right in line.

"We are not pincushions."

"WE ARE NOT PINCUSHIONS!"

"We are not punching bags."

"Class, settle down."

"WE ARE NOT PUNCHING BAGS!"

Brad Canby banged on his desk.

"We are not puppets."

"WE ARE NOT PUPPETS!"

"Class!"

"We are not pets."

"WE ARE NOT PETS!"

"We are not pawns."

"WE ARE NOT PAWNS!"

"We are people."

"WE ARE PEOPLE!"

"Louder! We are people."

"WE ARE PEOPLE!"

"*Louder!* We are people!"

"WE ARE PEOPLE!" the class shouted.

"We are people," Miles said, grabbing his bag and exiting the classroom, leaving the door wide open behind him.

## ACKNOWLEDGMENTS

There were so many people who helped and encouraged me in the making of this book. From my agent, Elena Giovinazzo, to the whole Disney Hyperion team, including Emily Meehan, Hannah Allaman, and Tomas Palacios. The Marvel team. Of course, the creator of Miles, Brian Michael Bendis. My buddies Adrian Matejka, Bonafide Rojas, Melissa Burgos, Jenny Han, Amy Cheney, and Lamar Giles. Brian Jacob at *The Ultimate Spin*. My high school English teacher, Ms. Blaufuss. My family. Brooklyn. Washington, DC. And all the Miles Morales fans who have cheered me on in this process. Thank you all for being the lifeblood for such an incredible part of my journey.